# TITANLORD

## A THOUSAND ASHES

Direct sequel to Titanlord: Of Death & Sacrifice
(Book 2 of the Titanlord Series)

M.G. DARWISH

TITANLORD: A Thousand Ashes
Text Copyright © 2020 by M.G. Darwish.

All rights reserved. Printed in the United Kingdom. No part of this book may be used or reproduced in any manner whatsoever without written permission except in the case of brief quotations embodied in critical articles or reviews.

This book is a work of fiction. Names, characters, businesses, organizations, places, events and incidents either are the product of the author's imagination or are used fictitiously. Any resemblance to actual persons, living or dead, events, or locales is entirely coincidental.

www.mgdarwish.com

Cover design by Nathaniel Dasco
ISBN : 978-1-7357411-0-9

# TABLE OF CONTENTS

OTHER BOOKS BY M.G. DARWISH .................. vii
PROLOGUE ....................................................... 1
CHAPTER 1 ....................................................... 8
CHAPTER 2 ..................................................... 12
CHAPTER 3 ..................................................... 33
CHAPTER 4 ..................................................... 36
CHAPTER 5 ..................................................... 41
CHAPTER 6 ..................................................... 51
CHAPTER 7 ..................................................... 58
CHAPTER 8 ..................................................... 61
CHAPTER 9 ..................................................... 70
CHAPTER 10 ................................................... 81
CHAPTER 11 ................................................... 89
CHAPTER 12 ................................................... 95
CHAPTER 13 ................................................. 104
CHAPTER 14 ................................................. 107
CHAPTER 15 ................................................. 117
CHAPTER 16 ................................................. 125
CHAPTER 17 ................................................. 132
CHAPTER 18 ................................................. 146
CHAPTER 19 ................................................. 158

| | |
|---|---|
| CHAPTER 20 | 172 |
| CHAPTER 21 | 178 |
| CHAPTER 22 | 186 |
| CHAPTER 23 | 190 |
| CHAPTER 24 | 200 |
| CHAPTER 25 | 210 |
| CHAPTER 26 | 215 |
| CHAPTER 27 | 229 |
| CHAPTER 28 | 235 |
| CHAPTER 29 | 239 |
| CHAPTER 30 | 247 |
| CHAPTER 31 | 254 |
| CHAPTER 32 | 266 |
| CHAPTER 33 | 273 |
| ACKNOWLEDGEMENTS | 279 |
| ABOUT THE AUTHOR | 291 |

## OTHER BOOKS BY M.G. DARWISH

Blood and Moon
(Fortier Book 1)

The Long Night: Blood Will Be Served
(Fortier Book 2)

Titanlord: Of Death & Sacrifice

This is dedicated to my wife, Z.

Thank you for agreeing to marry me -which delayed this release by at least 1 year.

I love you.

# THE WIDE SEA

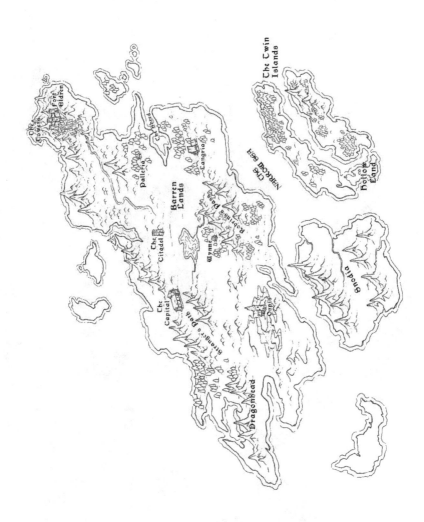

# PROLOGUE

A gentle breeze played on the people's face as it carried the sound of the oceans in its wake. People were flourishing as normal; mothers were tending to their children, while others were bargaining for a better price on the food they would devour later on.

The place was not small but wasn't big either. All the houses were located on either side, providing an equal view to a well that centered the village next to the townhall. Everything was made of pinewood, strong and sturdy enough.

A girl, no older than twelve, was pulling her mom towards a vendor that had a pretty blue dress on display. "Mommy, can I get this one?"

"No honey, I'm afraid we can't afford that right now," the mother responded as she smiled nervously at the vendor.

"I hate you; you never get me anything!" the girl cried as she turned her face away from her mother with a stomp.

# TITANLORD

"Come on, Lizzy, your dad is waiting for us," the mother said as she began to walk away slowly.

"Rise to the evils at bay! Darkness is upon us!" a man bellowed, wearing a torn and ragged brown robe as he stood next to the well.

"Ah, not again. He does this every single day, won't he tire or something?" the mother said as she held her breath. "Come now, child, lest the weird man eats you," she warned, her daughter came running back to her mother's arms.

"Get a life!" the vendor shouted at him.

The man stood still for a moment. "A life?" he repeated as he slowly tilted his head towards the man. "No, not a life. You all should bow before the Titans so that they may save you from what is to come."

The vendor laughed. "Oh yeah? And what's to come, prophet?"

He was no prophet, yet within the Hollow Lands, everything that wreaked of religion and the mention of Titans would be enough to declare you a Teetan—those who worship the Titans—and a zealot at that.

Within a blink of an eye, the sky darkened as a loud bang of thunder tore it apart. "They're here," the false prophet quivered as he took slow steps backward, his head craned up at clouds forming above.

Then, a translucid circle began to form in the sky, the last bit of blue disappearing into a light gray. The circle itself began to emit strange dark beams that flowed down to the ground, bubbling up in a haze as it touched the dirt as though it was water falling from a waterfall.

Then the growls begun; a shape began to form from the sludge on the ground, the liquid oozed against their body form as they tried to rip out of it, though it seemed a bit thick. It took a few tries, but then those creatures emerged. Deformed and hideous, they were shorter than normal humans, and their skin was as pale as snow.

They had fangs in place of teeth, and the noise they made was enough to have the mightiest of heroes on the ground pleading for their lives.

Few became many, dozens became hundreds as they chased all the villagers and butchered them with ease. "Mom!" Lizzy cried as one of the beasts jumped on her mother.

"Keep running, child, don't look back. I'll be right there with you," the mother said as she choked back her cries for help. She wouldn't shout, lest her child look back and become a target.

The entire place was being devoured whole as the dark skies burned red. Cries of agony and terror filled the air. Blood had covered almost the entirety of the village. Where once was green, now red dominated.

The girl ran and ran until her legs couldn't carry her anymore. She stumbled to her hands and knees, tears in her eyes. She looked up for a sign from God, anything, or anyone. Instead, her gaze fell upon a man sitting atop of a hill, who had been carefully watching the scene below him. He saw it all, how the demons scattered the people and sent everyone to the afterlife.

The girl wanted to scream, she wanted to call for help, but what help could that person do from atop what seemed to her as the biggest mountain of all. The creatures caught up and then circled her. She closed her eyes and squealed, anticipating the worst.

Then she heard a thud, and the creatures raised their voices. She slowly opened her eyes and was struck back. The man she glimpsed atop the hill was now standing a mere two feet away from her. Did he jump? She wondered for a second but pushed the thought away. She was confused, although deranged and forced into a fight or flight mode, she couldn't make sense of it.

But what bothered her still was that the creatures had all kept away from him. They were growling, but it wasn't the sound something makes when looking upon its prey. The man wore normal clothes and was unarmed, so why were these terrible creatures so unnerved by him?

"You haven't changed a bit, Sir Knight," a stranger said as he slowly stepped towards the man. He was slim and wore a long dark robe that covered his entire body, topped with a matching hat.

"What do you want?"

"I only wish to remind you of the oath you took."

The girl's eyes darted between them, unaware what to

do. They spoke the same language as her, of that she was sure, but why would they simply come down and just watch this horror? Did they intend to help?

"Help us," the girl finally broke her silence.

The knight took a deep breath and sighed. He ignored her gaze all together, but felt disturbed.

"You knew it wouldn't be easy. You knew it right then and there, but if you choose to engage, and to partake again, then you know the price you will have to pay."

The knight shook his head. "Is this the world I fought for?" he asked.

"No," the stranger said as the stranger's dark hair shook as he shrugged. "But it's the only one we have." As the stranger finished his words, the creatures jumped at the little girl and sunk their teeth into her. Death didn't come quickly to the girl, and her screams of agony echoed into the dark skies.

The knight curled his hand into a fist and clenched hard enough that a bit of blood dripped down his knuckles.

"Put aside your emotions, you have done all you can. Now comes the big test. You thought casting the Titans was the hard part?" the stranger asked as he tipped his hat. "Fighting is easy. It's dealing with the consequences and the aftermath that gets to you."

"What has the world ever done to this girl?" the Knight asked, his fist remained shut still.

# TITANLORD

"Consider it a sacrifice... One... that must come to pass," the stranger stuttered. The life in the girl began to fade away with every passing moment. "Look, this is the lesser evil, a path to the greater good. To the future we've dreamed of, and the one you can still bring to life."

The Knight couldn't see the girl as he shut his eyes, but his heart felt her pain as if it was his own. He could guess what they would bite next, and how she would die slowly and painfully, but for what? His hands trembled as he squeezed shut his eyes and his pale skin shivered at the thought.

"Colossal..." the stranger muttered.

"Evil is evil," the Knight said as he finally opened his eyes. The tension rose in the air and became so thick he could almost cut it in half with only his gaze.

The creatures immediately retreated as if his glare was enough to push them far away from the girl. The Knight began to walk slowly towards the edge of the village, surveying the destruction the demons created. "If the path to the greater good is through evil, then I'd rather have let the world burn."

The stranger shook his head. "Where are you going?"

The Knight turned slightly to look at him. "Can't you see? The Twin Islands are no more," he said as he kept on walking. "I'm going to Hollow Land."

"Why?" the stranger asked, his thick eyebrows furrowing together.

# M.G. DARWISH

"The future can catch up to me there."

The stranger covered his face with both of his hands in prayer. "May the Creator have mercy on us all."

# CHAPTER 1

## *The End Begins*

The Capital that was once a glorious sight to behold was no more. It laid in destruction and agony. The cries of children filled the restless skies as deformed creatures began to defile the lands. Tormented souls that were meant to remain banished wandered out in the open.

The demons cut through all; old, young, strong, or weak. Nothing halted them from executing God's justice as they began to initiate their plans of erasing mankind and starting the world anew.

Griffyn was running far away from the Capital. By some miracle, he had escaped with the sword that the Red Hand entrusted him with, the sword that harbored the only thing that could pose a threat to the Gods that descended: the Masamune.

Tears were running down on his cheeks as he flew past the terrified citizens. Those who stood their grounds and tried to fight for their right to live were being left for slaughter. Yet Griffyn did not wait, he did not fight back.

"Forgive me, forgive me," he repeated in agony as he rushed outside the keep and made his way through the courtyard. The demons that tore the place down seemed to ignore him as they had their jaws full of flesh. Griffyn ran and did not look back, the horrors trapped in his mind.

Within minutes, he was outside the once proud city that boosted its invulnerability. He paused as archers readied their arrows at him. Just outside, some of the remaining forces of the late King had rallied up and built a few barricades to keep the monsters at bay.

"Stop!" he shouted. "What are you all doing?"

"Hold your fire!" a voice commanded as he emerged into the light of the struggling sun. Squirmy eyebrows sat on a square face beneath a head of shiny golden hair. His eyes were a piercing light blue as he met Griffyn's gaze.

"Wilson?" Griffyn mumbled.

"What in God's name happened inside? What did you all do?" Wilson asked as he grabbed him by the shirt and pushed him around.

"Careful who you plead to. Gods are all out of mercy."

"Give me one good reason not to kill you where you stand," Wilson said as he sheathed his sword. "I take a chance on you, get you inside the city with that girl, and this is how you repay me? This is how?" he repeated, his face contorting in disapproval.

"It wasn't us."

"Then who was it? Point me in their direction, was it the Titans? Have they finally come for us?"

"We don't have time; we need to move. Run, please, take as many as you can. To stay here means absolute death," Griffyn rambled, as if the word 'Titan' had triggered the exact opposite reaction into his heart.

He shook his head. "You're a boy, and a coward at that," he growled before pointing at his sword. "You wield such a magnificent sword, yet you don't look like you can use it. Say, you didn't have this when you first came in, where did you get it?"

"There is no time, we have to run. The strongest people in the world weren't enough to stop them, and you and I are no Rory or Benjen," he cried as he fell to his knees, new tears appearing in his eyes. "They were my friends, and they all perished."

Wilson took a good look at the young man bawling at his feet. "Tell me what you saw in there, boy."

Griffyn shook his head. "Why are the brave ones always rushing to meet their end?"

"Because war does not spare the brave, but the cowardly," he whispered, just enough so he could be heard. "You of all people should know that."

They both lingered for but a moment when an ungodly noise tore through the walls and split the sky above. "What the hell is that!" Wilson shouted as he covered his ears. He turned and ran towards the barricade, but a sudden wave of light began to emerge from inside. He averted his eyes and squinted hard enough to make the details. It was a giant wall of flame, growing bigger and rapidly with every second, and it was coming right towards them.

Wilson stood frozen in his spot. The wall of flames was at least ten feet tall. There was no escaping it. "By the Gods, what is that!" he shouted as his eyes shut. It would be only moments before they were all reduced to ash. Or so he thought, as he began to gently whisper a few prayers of his own. A giant ruckus suddenly came from beside him. His eyes shot open to find the flames gone. Griffyn stood in front, where the wall was supposed to be, his sword in the air.

"Did you... do that?" he stuttered.

"Please, let's get the hell out of here," Griffyn pleaded before he collapsed to the ground.

# CHAPTER 2

## *Hope*

Griffyn opened his eyes lazily. He was laying in a bed made of straws, some sharp ends poking into his back. Looking at his surroundings, there was little he could make out from it. He didn't remember how he got to this point, but alas, all he did know was that he was in a tent.

He got up and looked around for his sword but didn't see it. His heart began to race as he searched the small room, but it was nowhere to be seen. The tent flaps whipped around him as he exited, and there the sword laid, against a boulder just outside, and rushed to inspect it. At first glance it seemed perfectly fine, so he rushed over to examine it more closely.

"You're finally up," Wilson said as he approached. "Nifty little sword you have there."

"What do you mean?" Griffyn shifted his feet.

"It looks ordinary enough that no idiot would try to steal it, but its edges are sharp enough to cut through steel."

"That's absurd."

"As absurd as the power that dwells within it, I'm sure," he said before pausing. He took a few steps towards Griffyn. "Somehow, you saved us back there. I meant no disrespect—"

"I wouldn't have believed me either."

Wilson smiled. "Now come, eat, and let us talk while you do so."

Griffyn followed him towards the center of the camp. He gazed across the field, and all he could see were trees surrounded by lush bushes. "Where are we?" he asked as the two of them sat by a cooking pot resting on a fire.

"We made camp just north of the Capital. This is Robrin's Pass, I believe."

"And the Capital?"

"Nothing. If that fire came from inside, then..." he couldn't finish, his face growing grim.

Griffyn sighed. "Everyone's dead."

Wilson raised his head a bit and scowled at him. "Is it easy for you? To talk about the dead this way?"

"You didn't see what I saw inside. We're human and

that is our weakness," he said as he gazed into Wilson's eyes.

"What did you see?" Wilson said as he took a bowl and filled it with soup. He grabbed a spoon and sipped on the hot meal. "Don't let me stop you. Go ahead."

"The Gods came down. They killed the King, his daughter, my friend and Ben..."

"Ben? As in Benjen Daguth? The Red Hand?" Griffyn's brows narrowed. "You knew him?"

Wilson smirked. "Knew him? I fought him in the rebellion twenty years ago. Such a formidable foe like him was unimaginable. Yet, I could guess this is the first time you have heard his full name, isn't it?"

Griffyn nodded.

"I'm not surprised. The Crown did all it could to distort the truth. They tried to erase all records that mentioned him or his ancestry everywhere, lest his story motivates another to take his place."

"They all died, Wilson, all of them. The Red Hand included," Griffyn repeated, his eyes filled with sorrow.

Wilson gritted his teeth. "So, you say we're fighting against the Gods, is it?" Griffyn nodded. "You might need to change the story a bit. If we are to garner support against them, you should try to liken them with barbarians or something more... ordinary."

"Fight them? Did you not hear me? There is no winning here, only death."

He shook his head. "What are you talking about? You survived them, tell us how."

"I don't know..." he said as he clicked his tongue. He grimaced as blood rushed through his cheeks. His brows touched and sweat began to form on his forehead. "I don't know..."

Wilson took a good look at him, and then lowered his gaze. "I understand, you know," he said as he paused, fiddling with his soup, and taking a deep breath. "I know it's not easy to talk about, but right now you're our best hope to understand how the Capital fell."

Griffyn buried his head between his arms, reluctant to give him an answer. "The sword."

"The sword?"

"It's the only weapon that can hurt them."

"And why is that?"

"I don't know."

"Dammit," Wilson said as he struck his knee with his palm. "You hold the answers, boy, you do. No matter the consequences, no matter what happened, you are the key to our salvation, whether you like it or not."

"Captain!" shouted one of the soldiers as he neared.

"What?"

"Our scouts returned. There are reports of a huge fire consuming a village not too far from here."

# TITANLORD

"What village?"

"It's called Wynne—"

You must go there. Griffyn heard the whispers inside his head. "Who are you!" he shouted. "What do you want!" His fingers clutched the sides of his head as he tried to get rid of the voice.

Wilson dropped his bowl of soup and tried to pull Griffyn's arms away. "Hey, hey," he soothed as he struggled to keep him from injuring himself. "Look at me," he added. "What's wrong?"

"The voices..."

"What voices—"

"Captain Wilson!" said another soldier that was rushing towards them. An iron helmet was all that they could see, aside from the deep blue eyes that sat within them. "We're under attack!" the soldier cried as a loud horn thundered across the camp.

The soldiers raced around the entire camp, as the thuds from their steps echoed across. They were preparing for battle. Some carried swords while others readied their spear.

"By who?" Wilson asked.

"...They're..." the soldier stumbled.

"Demons," Griffyn finished as he stood and picked up his sword.

"No," Wilson said as he turned towards him.

"I'm the only one—"

"You're only a child, you will sit back and wait. Is that clear?" Wilson insisted as he faced the soldier. "Report."

"They're surrounding us. It's as if we're facing off against a general of our own. One thing is clear, Captain; they're not using the usual simple tactics!"

"We need to set up a perimeter, ten paces. Spears in front, swords on the sides."

"That won't do," Griffyn said as he tried to interrupt.

"When did you become such a confident strategist?" Wilson asked as he turned his gaze away from him and took a step forward. He then halted. "Soldier, you are to babysit him. Do what you must to keep him safe, but you are not to engage. Is that clear?"

"Why?" Griffyn said as his eyes widened.

"Yes, Captain," the soldier obeyed.

Griffyn simply stood there, sword in hand, but couldn't make anything of it. Those moments were about the heaviest ones he felt in a very long time. His eyes watered, and he felt the urge to weep and fall to the ground, but nothing would come out.

"I know how you feel, if that makes it any better," the soldier said, removing his helmet. Dark brown hair came dipping onto her shoulders as water does in the deepest ocean. She offered Griffyn a hand. "Leah Pilthiel."

Griffyn pondered for a moment. He didn't shake her

hand, but he tilted his head and looked her in the eyes. "Tell me, Leah," he said before he took a pause. "Have you ever seen the person you love, and the person you grew up cherishing, be put to the sword right in front of you?

"Have you ever been in the position where you couldn't help, even if you wanted to? Have you ever killed someone you were raised alongside with your own hands?" he added.

"You may not think so, but there are more horrible crimes that wars have spurred about," Leah said as she flipped her hair over her shoulder. He killed someone with his own hands? She thought to herself.

"Come," she beckoned as she made way towards an open tent. "Now!" she shouted. His steps felt heavy, but he finally obliged. He went inside and found there was nothing, save for two benches and a bedroll.

They sat still. Leah didn't know how to talk to him, and he didn't feel like talking, not after what he had seen. She noticed that his head was casually falling down only to be lifted at the last second.

"How long has it been since you really last slept?"

"I don't remember," he muttered without shifting his gaze.

Leah sighed and sat close to him. "You can sleep. We'll keep you safe. That, I promise."

Griffyn made a hissing noise with his tongue. "The last

time someone swore to keep me safe, they broke their vow and are no longer alive."

"Stop it!" she shouted, causing him to jump back. "Whatever you are feeling, know that it'll pass, but not if you dwell on it every waking moment."

He shifted his head, only a little. She was getting to him. "And how do you know that? How do you know that the end hasn't begun?"

"We're here, aren't we?" Leah said, the words sending shivers down his spine. His face twitched, and she pressed it against her chest. "It's okay, it's okay," she repeated as he wept.

"I let them all die," he said, his voice muffled. "And I watched my best friend kill herself-"

"Let's talk about something else, shall we?" Leah pleaded, and Griffyn nodded. He glanced at her from the corner of his eyes, pulling himself away from her. He desired to have a normal conversation, more than anything at this time.

"Tell me about where you're from," Leah asked.

Griffyn looked her in the eye and didn't blink. "It was ravaged by a demon army."

Leah wiped the sweat that formed on her forehead. "Goodness," she mumbled. "How about I talk and you listen? Would that be okay?"

Griffyn nodded as he rested his head against the wall

of the tent. He closed his eyes and quickly opened them so he would not fall asleep.

"I'm not from the mainland. I'm actually from a place called Snodia. Do you know where that is?" Leah asked as she turned her head towards him.

He shook his head.

"Snodia is a separate country that is a bit far from here. It's directly south of the capital, but you can't get there by boat, not directly anyway. The northern region is marked by tall mountains that are said to rival those at the Towers."

"The Towers?" Griffyn asked.

"It's the furthest northern point on the Mainland. It houses some abandoned forts—"

"Fort Eldren?" he questioned.

"How do you know that?" Leah wondered.

Griffyn gawked at her. He couldn't tell soldiers of the imperial army that Fort Eldren was home to the remaining soldiers who followed the sworn enemy of the crown, even when no King ruled over. He felt it best to leave some details unanswered. "When I was in the village, we used to talk about it a lot."

"Ah" Leah said. She didn't mean to pry further, or to induce more pain when he was trying to heal. "Well, the area that houses all those great mountains is called the Towers. The legend says that the highest mountain touches the whisks of the heavens."

"That's ridiculous."

"That's why it's just a legend," Leah laughed. "I'm from a town called Brekk, which was built at the edge of a mountain slope."

"How's the weather there?" Griffyn pondered out loud, enjoying the distraction.

"It's dusty, humid and is technically a giant beach. It's not as big as the Mainland, but it has its charm."

"So why did you leave?"

"I left because I wanted to change something," Leah said as a sigh escaped her and her eyes softened. "I wanted to leave an impact on the world. I was young, but not naïve. I knew that the world needed some sorting out to do—"

"And the way to do that was to join the imperial army?"

"I know what you're thinking. King Magmar had many flaws, true, but no system exists that is perfect. So, I wanted to change things from the inside, and not like the rebel."

Griffyn pulled himself up and sat right. "That rebel was all that stood against us and something greater that wanted to reduce this world to ashes," he said as he jumped up and stood in front of her.

"You can blame the rebel, and you can even hate him, but know that in humanity's darkest hour, it was his light

# TITANLORD

that shone the brightest," he protested as tears began to run down his cheeks. "And for some fucked up reason, he believes me to be..."

"To be what?" Leah pried as she leaned closer to him. "You can trust me. I won't report it to Captain Wilson. You have my word."

Griffyn's heart pounded faster inside his chest. "Why would I do that?" he growled, sounding inhuman. "You lot fought the one who tried to save me and my friends, someone who died so that I may live, to learn the answer why..."

"Why what?" Leah insisted as she backed up again. "To learn what?"

He slowly tilted his head to the right, while fixating his gaze upon her. "Why the Gods themselves fear me and what I am."

Leah swallowed. "The Gods fear you...why? What do you mean?"

He shook his head gently. "There are so many questions, and so many ways to tell the truth, but in reality, the outcome is one; we are doomed, Leah," he said as he took a deep breath, closing his eyes. "There is no one strong enough in this world to stop what has come, what has descended."

Griffyn's thoughts were interrupted by the taste of Leah's cold palm against his face.

"How dare you say that?" she said as she got up and

pushed him away. "How dare you say that," she repeated. "It wasn't just you who lost your loved ones. You can't see that because you are a child, and I can let that go, but don't you dare mock the people who died fighting or those who are still fighting by saying that no one strong enough exists."

"Leah..." Griffyn mumbled.

"Can you really see nothing at all? You selfish idiot?" Leah snapped as she grabbed his shirt. It was torn, but she didn't mind it. He could use a new one by now anyway. "Can you not see that Captain Wilson hasn't given up? I haven't given up either. Why don't you see that? Huh? You survived whatever happened there, be it Gods or damned Titans, you of all people survived," she said, gasping to catch her breath between sentences. "So, don't you dare make a mockery of everyone who has survived so far."

Griffyn remained silent. His heart trembled, if only for a moment. She was right after all. He was still there, standing, even though those closest to him were not. "Who was it?" he asked.

"What?"

"Who was it that you lost?"

The words struck Leah as if a knife had entered her chest. "My...fiancé," she muttered as her heart ached. Griffyn had seen right through her anger. "I'm sorry—"

"I'm the one who has to apologize," Griffyn said as he

# TITANLORD

went and picked up his sword. "And you're right. We are still here, and as long as that holds true, then we keep on fighting."

"Listen, you can't join the fight—"

Leah's tongue went dry as a shiver went down her spine. The sword gave off a strange hew. The first orb that was encrusted in the sword's hilt glowed a deep orange.

"What is that..." she said.

"Please, don't stop me," he warned as he ran outside.

Leah caught up to him, pulling back on his arm. "You can't fight. Do you even know how to swing that thing?" she said. She turned her head to the skies and saw smoke filling the area.

"They are fighting Dwellers. They aren't like normal men. I've seen them..." he bit his tongue, "Twice. Once they surrounded the citadel and laid siege, and the second time was when the King was killed. They are not ordinary, and to defeat the extraordinary, you cannot be ordinary."

"You can't be a child either." Leah fought.

The sword glowed again. "I'm not a child."

"What am I to do with you?" Leah sighed.

"You said it yourself, it's not just me who has lost someone in this war, so let me fix it. Let me do something about it—"

"Why is he out of the tent?"

"Captain Wilson!" Leah said as she snapped up

straight.

"Did you finish them off?" Griffyn asked as he stepped closer.

Wilson turned to face a nearby soldier. "Get me a report on casualties right away, and make haste, we need to properly build a defense perimeter around the camp. Whatever those things tore at, I want fixed by sun fall."

"Yes, Captain!" the soldier barked as he marched away.

Wilson ignored Griffyn and began scanning his surroundings. "It seems that, by some miracle, they didn't reach here," he muttered as he stepped closer to Leah. "Your instructions were to keep the boy in the tent, was I not clear enough?" he asked.

Leah stood silent, her eyes cast down.

"I was the one who ran outside. She tried to hold me down, but I was a quick one," Griffyn said as he stepped between them. "Don't punish her for mistakes not her own."

"You will only speak when you are asked to, do you get me, boy?" Wilson growled as he glared at Griffyn.

"I get it, you're upset. You've seen something you don't understand, but don't take it out on her."

Leah's face twitched. As Wilson exhaled from his nose, he said "You want to play soldier that badly? Fine, come then," he said as he stepped inside a circular spot on the ground. There was enough space to move freely. "Come and draw that sword of yours."

"Captain, this might not—" Leah tried to intervene, but Wilson wouldn't have it.

"Quiet!"

"Are you sure you want to do this?" Griffyn asked as he slowly walked towards him.

"It's time to teach you both proper manners and humility."

"I think we should move, Wilson, we don't have time for this." Griffyn noted.

"Did you learn that through the many years of fighting on the frontlines? Pace yourself and charge."

Griffyn took a deep breath and brought his left foot forward with the sword. Before he could charge, a sudden roar tore at the sky. Their heads snapped up to the darkened skies as the sound echoed, the clouds became deformed, and lighting began to weigh on the grounds below one clap at a time.

"Get everyone inside, right now!" Wilson commanded Leah.

"No, wait!" Griffyn said as he stepped closer.

"I don't have time for c—"

They were all interrupted as a dark goo fell from the sky to land on the grounds next to them. It was translucid and circular, yet its color was darker than they remembered the color black to be. A thud, and then a noise came from within.

"By all that is holy, what madness is this," Wilson muttered, sweat prickling his skin.

"Captain!" Leah cried as she unsheathed her sword and stood by Wilson, ready to protect and serve.

"Get behind me," Griffyn shouted against the raving winds.

A figure then emerged from the hole as if it was crawling its way up. The goo ebbed as the creature pulled its way onto the sizzling grass, the blackness taking on a reddish hue. A sudden wave of heat hit them when a crackling noise along with the creature surfaced fully. They all shivered as the sounds grated against their ears.

Deformed and hideous; they had no shape nor structure at first, but then, as if on cue, it all retracted to form a basic shape. Humanoid in nature, yet vile and wicked. Darkened skin, fangs for teeth. It was a sight Griffyn knew well.

"What are those things!" Leah asked, appalled at the sight.

"Dwellers, they were once human," Griffyn said as he prepared to swing that large sword of his.

"This is not right...this...this is not natural!" Wilson muttered under his breath. He didn't know if anyone heard him, but in the end, he didn't really care. What he was witnessing was something from his darkest nightmares.

# TITANLORD

Prepared to defend themselves, they took their stance across from the small group of Dwellers. A bead of sweat trickled down Griffyn's brow as he waited for them to attack. But they never did.

They formed a line, and then another thud echoed behind them. More creatures crawled out of the ooze, falling into place next to their companions. Wilson flinched as a sharp tone tore through the air. Someone, or something, was coming closer and closer.

"Who bears the Masamune?" a voice spoke in their tongue; it was as clear as day.

Soldiers surrounded the three as they heard the ruckus. Wilson signaled them off. Charging insanely like that would not end well, he thought.

"Who wants to know?" Griffyn demanded.

"Would you answer a fly if it demanded your name?" the creature said as he stepped towards them slowly but carefully keeping his distance. It was similar in figure to the other Dwellers, but this one was pale and wore golden armor that shined enough to cast a light against darkness itself.

"Is that meant to intimidate us?" Griffyn said as he sighed. "Those words are not yours to begin with, so why don't you use your own arguments next time?" he added.

The creature laughed. "Clever little boy you are, aren't you? You must be the one Nepherin told us about." The mention of that name sent a shiver down Griffyn's spine.

"How do you know him?"

"Nepherin?"

Griffyn nodded, his eyes stern and never leaving the creature's face.

The creature scratched the back of his head with both of his hands as he let out a deranged sigh. "He is our God. And yours. Fight it all you want, but when that moment seeps into the back of your mind, that you cannot fathom a fight against a perfect being, that is when you will get the urge to bow."

"My God?" Griffyn let out a small laugh. "Is that why he couldn't finish me off? A child? Is that why he hides in a castle while he sends his followers to do his bidding?"

"Do as you may, but you are mortal. And all mortals tremble before us," the creature fixed his cold hard gaze upon Griffyn.

Griffyn shook his head. "Mortal? No, not while I hold this sword," he said as he pointed the Masamune towards him.

"Do you even know how to use that?" the creature giggled as he took a step closer. The soldiers tensed up and took another step as well.

Griffyn raised his hand, signaling the soldiers to stop.

"Pity, such a pity that Pollus has chosen a wimp," the creature taunted, and the Dwellers around him began to growl. "They grow hungry, would you mind if they devour you?" he asked calmly.

The soldiers fretted. Griffyn could sense the doubt seeping into their souls. "Prepare for battle!" Wilson commanded.

Griffyn took a moment to look at their faces and realized that this was the very first time they have seen anything remotely close to this. He knew deep down that the one thing that makes humans great is also their biggest weakness. It is the fear that rules the heart, and he knew it was beginning to take hold of everyone.

Time slowed down for Griffyn. In a flash, he remembered how he stood there, idly in the throne room, as he watched his best friend fight Nepherin and be pulverized. He remembered how Nepherin proceeded to kill his village hero and forced them to be on the run. A sudden spark ignited inside his chest, and he swung the Masamune so fast that a giant wave of wind hit the Dwellers as if it was a tidal wave, knocking them all away, save for the one that spoke.

"Interesting," the creature said as he stood still against the raving wind that had hit his fellow Dwellers. "This is most troublesome. Every fiber of my being tells me to make quick work of you right this moment, but alas, it appears that your destiny is to not fall on this day."

"Provided you weren't a coward, yes, it would appear so," Griffyn taunted him. He didn't know why, or how he moved his hands, but the time for words was done.

The creature lifted his hands to prepare for battle, but then a force began pulling him into the ground. "My God, I answer thy will," he said as he slowly oozed underneath the dirt and disappeared.

Griffyn took a hard breath, swallowing the lump in his throat.

"What in the world..." Wilson mumbled, his eyes and jaw wide open. "What...was that?" he asked.

Griffyn sheathed the Masamune and turned towards him. He used both of his hands to push him back. "Do you see what I mean? Do you see why I insisted to fight?"

Wilson remained quiet.

"How many?" Griffyn demanded.

"How many...what?"

"How many soldiers did you lose?"

Wilson glanced at a nearby soldier.

"Around a dozen, Captain..." the soldier replied.

"Dammit, Wilson!" Griffyn shouted. "Those lives were needlessly sabotaged because your damn pride got in the way. Their deaths are on—"

"Enough, Griffyn!" Leah interrupted. Her face was pale, but her tone was fierce. "Can't you see that the Captain is at a loss as well?"

"You too!" Griffyn shouted back at her. "Had I been fighting on the day you lost your fiancé, he would still

# TITANLORD

draw breath—"

Leah moved fast and slapped him before he finished the sentence. She simply eyed him up and down, her eyes swollen and her face red as the fury of the sun above them.

Griffyn took a hard glare at her, and then looked at Wilson. He turned his back and walked to the tent.

# CHAPTER 3

## *Rise*

Everything seemed translucent. An air of mystery hovered and surrounded him as Griffyn opened his eyes. He sat on a chair that rivaled the color of snow, and it was as if he could see the very air that was moving in front of his face.

He tilted his head and noticed a crowd had gathered before him. He was sitting not on a chair but rather a throne. "Where am I?" Griffyn gawked.

A man stepped forth, draped in a red silken robe. "You are now ready to bear the gift of the Voice."

"Who are you?"

"I am Veda."

"As in... the one in the chant? Veda, Pollus, Magnus?"

The man smiled. "That is for humans to decide who of

us they turn to at the turn of the tide. Once we were many, but now we are few. Those recitations carry not the purpose of our existence, but it alludes to the strongest amongst us."

"I... don't understand."

"It's fine if you don't, but the power that was bestowed upon you is calling to you."

Griffyn remained silent. He leaned backward and his eyes fell upon the Masamune. The sword glowed a bright blue for a moment. "It glowed just now, but it was a different color then before."

"Orange is the color of Pollus, blue is mine," the man said as he looked back. "Behold, a thousand ancient lords, who have all bled and led their people to victory again and again, all prepared to swear fealty to you." The man swept his large arm to the crowd in front of them.

Griffyn was shaking. He hadn't forgotten what he lost, but the final words that the Red Hand had uttered haunted him. His belief in him that, somehow, he was the one to save them all confused and irritated him. "How am I supposed to fight the Gods when the Red Hand couldn't?"

The man shook his head. "The Red Hand... had only one Titan Power. You have both," he signaled with his hand and all the lords gathered in the hall kneeled before Griffyn.

"We swear fealty to you. From henceforth, you are our Lord, and we are your protectors. From the depths of the

Darkness, will we lead you into the Light."

Those voices echoed in the back of his mind. The man stepped forward again. "Rise...Titanlord."

# CHAPTER 4

## *Darkness to Light*

His clothes clung to his wet skin as Griffyn gasped. "Was that really a dream?"

"You're finally up," Leah said as she appeared beside him. He was laying on a bedroll inside the tent that he hid in during the attack.

Griffyn scratched the back of his head. "From the depths of darkness, will we lead you into the light."

"What?"

"Does that mean anything to you?"

Leah leaned closer. "That sounds like something one of those Teetans would say."

"What do they even know of the Titans they worship?"

"They believe. What they know does not matter," she said before she sighed. "Black suits you," she shot him a compliment as she eyed him up and down.

Griffyn lowered his head and noticed that his torn rags had been exchanged for a black tunic. "Who-how...what..." he fumbled as blood rushed to his cheeks.

"You collapsed. I think fatigue was catching up to you. Well, no matter—"

"I know what I have to do, Leah," Griffyn said as he looked at his hand. "I'm sorry about what I said earlier. No, let me finish. It's not been easy for me. I feel terribly alone and empty inside, but for some weird reason, when I faced those Dwellers, my loneliness was devoid...as if I was closer to Rory, Vendel, and Ben when I... acted like them."

"They say that imitation is the highest form of flattery."

"That's all good and well, but I am not fierce as Rory, nor as brave as Ben, so I'll have to find my own way to fight, but I think I won't give up."

Leah leaned closer. "Don't think," she said as she grabbed his hand and folded it into a fist. "Honor their sacrifice, hold their memory close to you, and turn them into your weapons."

It was as if a giant sword had pierced his heart, and he choked back tears. "Does it get any easier?"

Leah shook her head. "You just get stronger," she said

as she sat next to him. He instinctively pushed his head against her shoulder, and she embraced him.

"It's too heavy, Leah...I feel it every second, as if a hole is widening up in my soul."

"Let's just sit this through a bit."

"How did you do it?"

Leah paused and looked him in the eye. "By not being consumed by what I lost. Instead, I asked myself this: what remains?" she explained as she pulled on his thumb.

Griffyn's eyes felt heavy. He pushed his index finger out of Leah's grip. "Natasha, and Dale, and Tatiana, and..."

"You have me, and Captain Wilson, whom I think is growing fond of you-"

They were interrupted by footsteps as the Captain entered. "Leave us."

"Yes, Captain," Leah barked as she stood up and tried to leave. Griffyn held her hand.

"Can't she stay?"

"No," Wilson's tone brooked no argument.

Leah made her way out, but not before she slipped a smile at Griffyn.

"She likes you," he said as he stood next to Griffyn.

"I like her too."

A smirk took shape on his face. "I've not the faintest idea what to do. That is the truth."

"You agree now that taking the capital is not viable?"

He nodded. "There's an army of demons in the capital, and a fire rages on in a village to the southeast. What has become of the world, I do not know."

"You don't have to understand evil," Griffyn said as he got up. "We need only to fight. To take back our lands and strike those who have harmed us and killed our friends."

"What do you think we should do?" Wilson prodded.

"Me?" He pondered for a moment. "We should ride to the village and see if there's anything to be saved."

Wilson balled his fingers into fists. "And if demons reign there? What becomes of it if we save it?"

Griffyn staggered but said nothing in response.

"Who rules over it? By whose authority do we march there?"

Griffyn's brows narrowed. "You asked me what I thought we should do."

Wilson shook his head. "I'm trying to teach you something. It's not enough to barge head first into a situation without thinking of the consequences."

"But is that really grounds to stand still and let everyone die?"

Wilson took another step towards him, lowering himself. He grabbed Griffyn's arms. "The King is dead. Demons are torching the mainland as we know it," he said as

# TITANLORD

he took a pause. "What do you think will happen to them if we just kill whoever is attacking and leave?"

Griffyn took but a moment as his eyes widened. "Chaos."

"Chaos," Wilson repeated, though his heart kept racing. He released his hold on Griffyn. "I didn't mean to ridicule, but when you stood up against that thing, when all of us froze, I saw something in you. And the young rush to a foolish death because—"

"They don't plan ahead." Griffyn finished for him.

Wilson nodded. He saw within the boy a man capable of standing against the atrocities. Was it wrong for him to pass the burden to a child? Even though that child may be the last hope for humanity?

"What do we do then?" Griffyn asked.

"We ride to Wynne."

"Wynne?"

"It's the village that is struck with fire at the moment. We leave at daybreak, though it is a short march from here. When we reach, we will—"

"Wait, after all that talk about not diving headfirst without a proper strategy..."

"I am showing you what a true commander should look like," he said as he turned around. "But sometimes, time is of the essence. And improvisation is as grand a trait as any," he finished before leaving the tent.

# CHAPTER 5

## *Vita*

Upon hearing a loud thud, Griffyn woke from a deep slumber. It was at the break of dawn when his pupils grew wide and opened. He stretched as much as his body would allow him; a black tunic, and his old pants. He scratched the inner corners of his eyelids as he yawned.

He wore his brown belt and tied the Masamune on his back. "I swear it gets lighter every day. This thing is cursed as much as it is blessed."

As he strode through the exit, the camp was a shell of what it was when he went to sleep. Soldiers were running around, buzzing like bees, taking anything with them that they could carry. They prepared logs and as much food as they could forage. "What is this," he gawked.

"Apologies, sir, Captain Wilson has ordered that you remain inside until notice is sent to you."

Did he just call me sir? Griffyn thought to himself. "Well, Captain Wilson informed me yesterday that I was to observe as much as I desired. To have me learn, so that I may rule one day," he said as he touched the soldier's shoulder.

"Yes, sir," the soldier frowned but didn't want to take the risk.

"What's your name by the way?" Griffyn asked.

"Cory, sir."

"Do you mind if I ask a few questions, Cory?"

The soldier shook his head.

"What is happening here exactly?" Griffyn asked as his eyes were bewildered with the organized chaos. Everyone seemed to know exactly what to do. They moved so smoothly, and he felt that if they wanted to construct the most complex of buildings, it would take only a few hours, not weeks, with this kind of discipline.

"We are preparing to march immediately."

"But that doesn't look like an army preparing to attack."

"That's because they aren't planning to," said a familiar face as she strode past the guards. "Is he bothering you, Cory?" she asked.

The soldier shook his head politely.

"Yes, Cory, am I?" Griffyn said as he turned towards the soldier. He saw the sweat pile up on the soldier's forehead before he was snatched by Leah.

"What! I was just having some fun!"

"The Captain ordered that you must be kept safe no matter the cost. That is why the soldiers are being nice to you, but you shouldn't let that get into your head."

"Always so...preachy."

"Uh huh." A smile crept onto her lips at that.

"Wait, if we aren't planning to attack, then what are we going to do?" Griffyn asked.

"The Captain doesn't share his battle plans with soldiers, you know. All we know are whispers."

"What are you talking about, he looked me straight in the eye last night and told me we are marching to Wynne."

Leah stopped. "Look at everyone. They're tired, and they've just witnessed demons for the first time in their lives. Do you think it wise to ride straight into war in this condition?"

"I don't mean to be a prick, but what choice do we have?"

"I suppose we're heading to Lake Vita first."

"Lake Vita?" his eyebrows furrowed together in confusion.

"You...have you ever been anywhere? Like ever?"

# TITANLORD

"I'm... not really well traveled in the sense."

"Well, if you are going to lead someday, you need to understand a few concepts about war and strategy. Namely, it's no easy task to mobilize a force without access to resources."

"So, we're heading to Lake Vita, restock on water, and then head to the village?"

"Now you get it." Leah smiled at him.

"Why couldn't you say that from the start?"

"Because some answers are worth getting yourself."

"But if you have the knowledge that I lack, why should I strive the same as you to get the same answer when I could be answering another question that hasn't been tackled yet?" he retorted.

"Griffyn, please, I have a short temper."

"Fine," he shrugged. "There's Wilson."

"Captain!" Leah shouted as she saluted him.

"Back to formation, we are moving out," he said to her as he turned his eye towards Griffyn. "I had a little run in with the guard assigned to your tent."

"Cory? He is a great guy. Hope he didn't bother you with nonsense."

"You're too impulsive," Wilson shrugged as he walked closer to an open area. He drew his sword. "Come," he commanded as he took his stance.

"What's that supposed to prove? That you can beat a child?" Griffyn mocked as he stepped closer to him.

"If you want to be more involved, then now is as good as any time to practice whether your sword can match your silver tongue," he challenged.

"I've never used a sword before. This is hardly fair."

"You would shout about unfairness when you look upon the Gods that have taken the lives of your friends?"

"Stop it," Griffyn's face flushed and his blood heated at Wilson's words.

"You think anyone cares if you're a child or not? If you wield a sword, learn how to use it."

Griffyn took a deep breath. He knew that this was a weakness of his, and one that his enemies would not shy away from using. He had to learn to control his rage that was building as images grew in the back of his mind of Nepherin, the King of the Gods, as he laid the commands to take out his friends.

His pupils dilated and glowed orange for a moment before reverting back to normal. He charged at Wilson, swinging the Masamune left and right.

Wilson parried and dodged to the right as he struck him with his elbow. Griffyn stumbled forward to the ground from his momentum. "Don't rush like a mad goat. Think before you attack, think!" he instructed as he waited for him to get up.

Griffyn got to his feet and readied himself. He sighed

and closed his eyes for a moment. All it took was an instant. It is about technique and form. The basics are: upper right, upper left, right cut at the middle, left, then lunge. He had once heard Rory recite those words to Vendel, and if it was anyone's form that he would try to imitate, it would be that of the most valiant warrior he had ever seen.

He tried to use the basic form as best he could. He rushed it. However, Wilson saw through the basic attacks and kept parrying each of his hits. "You're too green to fight in a war. How would you fare against the Gods then, huh?" he mocked.

"Stop..." Griffyn pleaded as he swung endlessly, his breath coming shorter.

"Make me," Wilson commanded as he took an extra step back, leaving Griffyn breathing heavily. "The weak have no right to make requests of the strong."

"It is not by weakness that I plead, but rather with justice," Griffyn replied as he looked at him from the corner of his eyes.

"Yet, you remain weak. And the weak cannot do anything about justice."

"To hell with your games," Griffyn spat as he threw down the Masamune. He stood idle, absent thoughts of tyranny and injustice in his mind; he remained a boy, nonetheless.

Wilson rushed towards him, picked up the sword, and slapped his face so hard that blood rushed to his cheeks.

The hit forced him to pause and wonder what had just happened.

"Never, and I mean never, throw down your sword," he said before leaning closer to him. "You like to act all tough and smart when it just suits you, don't you? Well what about us, huh? What about the people who rely on you to be strong enough?" he added before he took a breath. "This isn't a choice anymore, Gods or Titans be damned, you are the key to our salvation. You need to stop acting like a boy."

"Maybe I should spend my time with better people," Griffyn replied as he took his sword from Wilson and started walking away. He made his way towards the middle of the camp, where once the tents were. Everything was getting ready to be mobilized on a large scale.

"Griffyn?" A familiar voice shouted.

"Leah," Griffyn said as he moved charging towards her.

"What happened?" she asked.

"What do you mean?"

"Your face is fuming, your grip on the sword is a bit tighter than usual, and where I just left you, you were sparring with the Captain. So, what happened?"

"He just doesn't get it," he shouted as he turned his face away from her.

Leah smiled. "Come with me for a second," she said as she pulled him away from the commotion and towards a big tree that hung on the outskirts of the camp.

"I know he's your captain and all, but has he no heart?" He said as he took cover in the shade.

"He sees something in you," she replied and sat beside him.

"I don't care. To hell with what he sees, to hell with it all!" He cried as he clenched his hand into a fist. "It's always the same shit, 'I see something in you, so I will be rude and heartless.' Don't they ever think that compassion goes a longer way than fear and intimidation?"

"You wouldn't say that if you were in his position," she said as she squinted her eyes at him. "Look at you. You're a boy, Griffyn, but you wield the only weapon that may save us all. That's hard on him, you know."

"He hates me because I am better than him."

She shook her head. "He hates the fact that he has to throw you into this life, that he cannot bear the burden off of you. And so, he helps in the only way he can; training you."

"Well then, his way is wrong. Just because he was trained a certain way, doesn't make it the right one for me."

"Yes, that is so, but how do you expect him to know better?"

"It's not what I expect of him, Leah. Dammit, can't I just do it my way?"

"Sure, tell me about your way. What would you do?"

Griffyn went silent, his eyes on the charred ground as he thought. "I'd train, and then—"

"Challenge the Gods? Train how, and in what way? Warriors spend lifetime's training to be as good as the Captain is with a sword, and he froze when he saw the Dwellers."

"Yes, I get that..."

"Do you?" she asked before she got up. "He's being tough on you because every day you remind him that his power alone isn't enough, and you aren't enough."

Griffyn remained silent. He knew that it was true deep down in his heart, that his power alone would not be sufficient.

"You're a good person, Griffyn, but good can only take you so far."

"That's repulsive to me," his face contorted in disagreement.

"What do you mean?" she shrugged.

"Good is, and will always be, enough. Evil is evil, no matter how you look at things, or how you try to label them as lesser or greater."

Leah smiled. "That is why one day you will be a leader."

"Why?" Griffyn said as he stood up. "Because I believe in what should be the norm? Then how awful it is for the rest of us, if one should only behave how they should've in the first place to be a leader?"

"The world seems so simple to you now, but wear the crown on your head, and all is shifted."

"Then I'd rather toss the crown in the trash."

Leah shook her head, her hair bouncing. "There is no winning with you, is there?"

"I have a method in which I operate, Leah. That method is how I view the world and how I think. I'm not about to cast that aside for something so trivial like that."

"Like I said, the world isn't so simple—"

"Why not? Why is it that we adapt to the complexity of the world around us? Don't we ourselves shape it in the first place?"

"You have your way, I'll give you that..." Leah sighed as she looked up.

"Move out!" they both heard the command finally be given to march towards Lake Vita, then from there to Wynne.

"Come on, let's get going."

# CHAPTER 6

## *Oath*

Serenity waited across the mainland. On a small island that housed no cultures nor wildlife, sat a man gazing at the lonely stars above. He wore a white tunic and dark leather pants. He seemed lost in his thoughts, until he heard footsteps that disturbed his peace and quiet.

"Colossal?" said the intruder.

The man didn't budge, as if he hadn't notice.

"It has begun. It is your duty as a knight to—"

"Why?"

"I beg your pardon?"

"Why is it that you disturb my peace, even in Hollow Land."

# TITANLORD

"You know why," the stranger said as he stepped closer to him. "Do you know why it is called Hollow Land?" he asked, but the knight wouldn't budge, let alone answer such questions. "It is said that an old Titan fell in love with a mortal, and upon her death, he came here. It was a utopia, filled with civilization, and he—"

"Pierced the ground with his palm, eradicating all life," The man finished for him, irritation dripping in his voice.

"So, you are a student of history."

"What do you want, Ceris?" the Knight finally asked. "Really, no tricks, no games and none of your damn puzzles."

Ceris took a moment to gather his thoughts. His black robe danced against the winds passing them by. "The world is ending..."

"So?"

"You helped prevent Armageddon before, why not join hands now and strike as one?"

The Knight took a deep sigh. "Humans are foul, and all of them show their true selves, come the right moment. Dwellers, Titans or Gods, they are no different. All desire destruction."

"What about you, the Great Colossal?"

"That is not my name."

Ceris shook his head. "It doesn't matter, but now, if

you two meet there is a chance to end the plague before it begins."

"And then what? Save the world again? So that the cycle repeats and another comes to strike at humanity once more when we are all returned to dust?" Colossal said as he got up and turned to face Ceris. "Tell me, old friend, why should I save a world I no longer have stakes in?"

"You don't know if he will turn or not."

"Just like I didn't know that the seal would break, that the Gods would descend, and that Dwellers would stalk the lands? Spare me your moralizing. What I saw was not a prediction, it was reality."

"Then change it, by all the Gods and Titans alike, by the Creator, change our reality. Help deliver us from the darkness before it plunges everyone into the pits..."

Colossal took a good look into his eyes. "The world can be damned," he said before he took a pause. "I am done saving a world that has shunned, betrayed, and forsook me."

"Then we are all doomed."

"Let the darkness come, for if I am too weak to help deliver light, then woe unto me."

Ceris stepped closer towards him and gently touched his shoulder. "Do you remember, during the war, what you said when you decided to follow me?"

Colossal laid silent.

"You said 'until I shape my perspective of the world

and what this all means, I'll follow the one man whose vision always transcended others.' Do you remember when you said that?"

"The war is over."

"No, old friend, the war merely paused, and now, it returns."

Colossal took a deep sigh and reverted his gaze back to the sky. "It's been a very long time," he muttered in awe of the horizon. "We were just kids playing at war back then."

"The pieces were not yet complete; we had no choice. Do you remember—"

"Didn't you have enough of the past already?" Colossal said as he turned to face him. "You keep mentioning things that you remember, but you forget one thing; the world has changed. Since the times of the great war, everything has changed. The world we set out to save and protect is no more. And it didn't take a dark lord to corrupt it all, it just took a man with an idea and a concept. Selfishness and greed destroyed the world long before the Gods possessed the rulers."

"You despise the past because it is true, and no matter what foresight you have, you can only gaze into the future and not the past. Yet, it is only those who learn from the past that grow to be strong enough to change the future."

Colossal let out a chuckle. "Go ahead, tell me what you remember, I'll listen," he said as he sat back down, crossing his legs.

"When we were at Robrin's Pass, and you made the decision to take on the rebels in open battle, no one dared to oppose you. Do you know why?"

Colossal shook his head.

"Because they believed in you, they saw something in you."

"Just as I saw in you?"

Ceris nodded. "You propelled us to this exact moment, this one reality where a man could strike a God and take back the world and reshape it entirely."

"And that man lays beneath the ground. The signs were clear; it was the dragon whom I was supposed to save, yet even he abandoned all and choose to save a world that forsook him."

"But the men fighting for him didn't," Ceris interrupted. "Can you not see? The Titanlord is not yet done for. We have hope—"

"Pathetic," Colossal said as he stood up. "You grow old, too old to inspire with just words of no meaning. You claim a dragon was not abandoned because he was surrounded by soldiers? Well, soldiers obey."

"Not exactly—"

"Stop retelling tales of the past and ancient glories, old man. You will find no listeners here," he said as he walked away from the hill.

# TITANLORD

"You will regret these words when the boy becomes a man. And I shall be there to remind you of your oath to stand by him."

"Then perhaps I should visit this boy and put an end to this madness all the same."

"You may strike him as he is now, but he shall become a legend, and legends never perish."

Colossal paused and turned. "You believe he will be stronger than me? Is that it? Provoking me into accepting to partake in a ridiculous crusade? Is that truly the grand scheme of Ceris the Cunning? Please, I've enough of this."

Colossal turned his back and focused his gaze upon the horizon. Though it was a parched wasteland, he found beauty in the silence that gloomed the lands. It was life as it was intended, undisturbed and left alone; not in the mercy of anything but its own fate.

Colossal crossed his arms, and slowly closed his eyes. Ceris gently touched his shoulder. "Colossal, don't."

Colossal then opened his eyes once more. "You're worried?"

Ceris swallowed the lump in his throat. As he averted his gaze, sweat began to form on his forehead. "Last you went to slumber, Titans were forgotten..."

Colossal grinded his teeth, and his head began to shake gently before settling. His pupils dilated and grew large enough in size that his blood vessels began to shine like the color of the sun. "So long as I live, Titans will never be forgotten," his tone quivered and faltered, as if he were hurt at the suggestion. He then closed his eyes once more.

# CHAPTER 7

## *Visum*

A clear day marked the army's march straight towards Lake Vita. Though it resided a few days away from the Citadel, Griffyn had never laid eyes upon it when he first traveled away from Palleria. Rory had ensured that they stayed away from the main roads. The place was spacious, though the army had stayed mainly in one mass, moving one step at a time. Griffyn had the time to gawk and look around the surroundings, appreciating the greenery.

There were trees as far as his eyes could see and lush grasses, save for the dirt path that made towards Wynne. Occasionally, his gaze would be disrupted as bird chirps would halt, and nearly all manner of animals would run the further the army marched.

"Halt."

A stranded voice commanded nearly the entire army. Many repeated the word, and then silence spread amongst their ranks. Griffyn pondered left and right. "Why are we stopping?" he said.

"Sir," a soldier said as he approached him. "Captain Wilson requests your presence immediately."

Griffyn nodded as he followed the soldier to the back of the army. There, Wilson waited on a magnificent white horse. As his eyes laid on him, he dropped down and stepped closer. "We are sending a scouting party ahead."

"Okay, that's a good plan."

Wilson's brows narrowed. "Idiot," he said as he moved past him. Griffyn followed, his face scrunching in confusion. "You are going to join the scouting party. Make sure to absorb as much as you can, but it is vital that you do not engage should you see anything or anyone. Is that clear?"

"You're sending me?"

"Would you rather I send another?"

"I'll do it," he shrugged as he made his way towards the front of the camp. There stood a few soldiers. He recognized the face of one. "It seems that fate has bound us together."

"Shut up," Leah said as she approached them. "Listen up, we're going to scout ahead. Scouting means information gathering. It doesn't mean-"

"Yeah, yeah, I've heard the lecture already. Can you

speed this up?" Griffyn interrupted.

Leah smiled, and stepped closer to him, until she was a step away. "When we're out there, I am not Leah, I am not your friend, I am your reporting officer. You will speak only when asked for your opinion."

"What if I spot an enemy?"

She took a deep sigh. "Griffyn, don't be a smartass."

"I'm not."

She shifted her gaze away from him. "Whatever you see or hear you report back to me immediately. If you see an enemy or two, do not approach. However, if you feel threatened, you may take appropriate action. Is that clear?"

All of the soldiers nodded and sounded their agreement.

"Move out," she demanded. The soldiers gathered walked along the road ahead for a bit before she noticed one had not moved. Griffyn stood there still.

"You too," she said.

"Leah, I just want you to know that I am being this difficult because I feel I can confide in you. You're a great person, and you'd sure make a great captain."

Leah scratched the inside of her ear, not sure she heard him right. "What?"

Griffyn shook his head. "Let's get going."

# CHAPTER 8

## *Ashes to Ashes*

Nozzles flared as the scouting party narrowed the distance between them and Lake Vita. The terrain was filled with lush grasses that flanked a narrow dirt path; this road was not built for armies. They marched closer to their destination until a tall tree watching over the wide lake came into view.

"We're here!" Griffyn shouted.

"Not so loud," Leah shushed him as she approached. "Do you even know what scouting means?"

"I know what it means, but there's no one here. I think it's safe," he said as he rushed towards the lake.

"Idiot," Leah mumbled before she signaled the others to join them. Griffyn immediately went to the lake and cupped his hands in the cold water, trying to get as much liquid inside them as he could hold. Yet, within the reflections of the water, he saw a shadow.

He quickly turned around. "You know I could see you all this time, right?" He snarled at Leah who attempted to scare him.

"If I wanted it, you would be dead already."

"Sure, whatever you say—" Griffyn paused. The world began to move slow around him as he turned towards Leah. Her words were muffled, like whispers, to his ears.

They're here. A voice said, loud and clear. "Who is it?" he asked as he shook his head trying to make sense of what was happening. "Who are you?"

"Snap out of it!" Leah shook him to his senses. "What the hell is wrong with you?" she added.

"You didn't hear that?" He looked at her with confusion clouding his eyes.

"Hear what?"

"Someone, or something... he said, 'They're here,' and it was as if they were talking right beside me."

"No one was near you. What are you talking about, who's here?" She squeezed his shoulders.

"Leah!" one of the soldiers shouted as he neared her.

"What's wrong?" She let go of Griffyn and turned to meet the soldier.

"There are these things... coming out of the ground!" The soldier stuttered as he drew his sword. Leah followed suit.

Command them. Griffyn heard the voice again as he laid his hand on the Masamune. "Wait," he said to them as he began to walk towards them. "Where are they?" he asked.

"Lieutenant?" the soldier glanced at Leah, who nodded. "They're coming from there," he said as he pointed south.

Griffyn's pulse rose as he drew his sword. Leah pushed his sword against him. "No, you won't attack. Just sit tight and close to me until we clear them out."

He shook his head. "I'm fighting."

Leah pulled him away from the group. "If anything were to happen to you, I wouldn't be able to face the Captain. So, just have faith in us."

He hesitated but nodded as he traced a few steps back. His only objective was to overlook this battle and how Leah, an experienced soldier, would lead this fight.

"Form a circle around us," Leah commanded. The soldiers obeyed without a second thought. No one objected, no one gave their thoughts, they just placed their complete faith in Leah's words...they entrusted her with their lives.

This is what being a leader means? He thought to himself. It wasn't long before the creatures came into view. The air around them grew dense and the tension rose amongst the humans. "Do not falter! You represent the light! And you shall pierce through the darkness and bring about a new day!" Griffyn shouted. They must be nervous, he thought. How those precise words came out of him, he didn't know, but it was those words that made the difference. The soldiers roared as the creatures halted.

"Everyone in front, charge!" Leah shouted as the soldiers covering their front rushed the creatures. A clash of swords against those ungodly beings followed, and where one fell, another took its place.

"There's no end to them!" one of them shouted.

"Press on!" Leah chimed in as she too drew her sword.

Leah gazed upon her soldiers, fighting bravely for their right to exist. "Fight!" she yelled as she was fixated on her men.

Griffyn grabbed her hand. "Order them to retreat, now!" he said, but Leah shrugged him off.

"Don't underestimate a trained soldier-"

She was cut off as one of the creatures sank their teeth into a soldier's feet. His cry shattered the air around him. Another soldier rushed to rescue him, but felt the cold sensation of iron deep within him. He looked down and one of the creatures had driven its long nail inside his chest. The soldier fell flat on his face, his heart stopping before he hit the ground.

The creatures devoured the wounded soldier. "Left flank, charge-"

"No! Tell them to hold their ground" Griffyn interrupted her. Leah, bemused, pushed him aside as she drew her sword and ran towards the creatures.

"Dammit, Leah," Griffyn shouted as he drew the Masamune. Before he could move an inch, he heard a loud noise coming from his right. "Shit, they're trying to flank us," he said as he looked towards Leah and then at the soldiers. Time slowed down and sweat began to form on his forehead. What do I do? he pondered for a moment before he tightened his grip on his sword and swung it. "Come on!" he shouted as he swung again.

"Come on, dammit! What good is Titan Power if I can't use it to save anyone-"

A loud scream came from the left; Dwellers had managed to reach their flank. They were slowly being encircled. He eyed Leah. She was fighting furiously, swinging her sword as though she was dancing, slicing through one Dweller and then another.

To his right, soldiers were fighting to keep the Dwellers from getting in between them, and to his left soldiers were being cut down by the Dwellers. He traced back towards the tree that had stood there against all strands of time.

"What do I do? Speak to me you damn voice... anyone!" he pleaded out loud hoping that the answer would come to him. "Behind you!" he heard someone yell. He turned around as a Dweller came straight towards him. Griffyn smiled as he spread his arms open and closed his eyes.

The Dweller charged and jumped into the air.

"Leah!" One of the soldiers yelled as he jumped in front of the Dweller.

Open your eyes, Titan. The voice commanded him.

He did as commanded and found the body of Cory laid before him. He walked slowly towards the Dweller who was trapped beneath Cory's body and struck its head. It squealed before dropping.

Before he knew it, half a dozen of them were rushing towards him. He readied his sword, and as one of them jumped towards his left, he swung against it, ripping its head off. He dashed to the right and struck another.

In a flash, he heard another squeal as he felt the back of someone press against his. He glanced from the corner of his eye just enough to make the details of who it was.

"Leah..." he mumbled.

"Shut up, keep your fucking mouth shut," she said as her voice broke apart.

"I'm sorry," he said as he swung the Masamune upwards and followed it with a left swing. As he was moving, he felt as if the sword was guiding him, showing him what he needed to do.

"You idiot," Leah said. She kept fighting on, but her voice was trembling. "While we are dying here to protect you, you do something so selfish?" she yelled as she added more power to her attacks.

"Calm down and focus, Leah, please," he said as he was engaged too, slicing whatever came in front of him.

Griffyn was preoccupied, too zoned in to fighting that he overlooked her for a moment. Then he heard her gasp. He turned around to see a few Dwellers holding her legs while the other shoved its long iron nails into her stomach.

"Leah!" he shouted as he barged towards her and swung the Masamune as hard as he could. It was only for a moment, but his pulse rose and his eyes glowed orange. A gust of wind came of out the Masamune and pushed the Dwellers away.

Griffyn rushed to her, dropped his sword, and picked up her head with his hands as he burst into anguished laughter. "This is the moment it works? Now?" he said, not slowing his laughter down.

"Are you okay?" Leah mumbled with a weak voice.

His laughter stopped as he screamed as loud as his lunges allowed him. He went silent for a moment, and then crumbled. "I'm fine, I'm fine, as useless as I am."

"Look around you," she said as she used what strength she had left to put her hand on his cheek. He felt the warmth of her touch, and as he raised his head, his eyes grew wider. All the Dwellers were staying back, growling and squealing at him.

"I...—"

"You really pissed me off..." she admitted before she

paused for a moment. "You don't get to give up. Ever, do you hear?" she said.

"What good is power if I can't use it to protect anyone," he wondered, and his eyes felt heavy.

"I'm pretty beat up; else I would've slapped you just now."

"Why?"

"Why?" she coughed. "Do you just want to feel sorry for yourself? Do you want to keep crying because of the past? Or will you be man enough to stand for the future?"

"It's not about that..."

"Then what is it about? Because right now, I am confused."

"I don't ever want to lose someone in front of me. You don't get it—"

They were interrupted as a loud horn blew. The sound of soldiers marching in a steady form grew louder with each moment. Griffyn turned his gaze away from Leah and saw the flags of the King. "Spears to the front!" the order was given. Though he didn't see him, he could make that tone and separate it anywhere. It was Wilson. Help had reached them.

A dozen soldiers marched ahead of the army all carrying long heavy spears. They held their weapons down and waited for further command. Griffyn's eyes widened as the Dwellers marched straight on ahead.

The soldiers, however, did not even flinch. As the Dwellers grew closer and closer, they jumped towards the spearmen. Then the order came from Wilson. "Now!" he barked, and the soldiers all raised their spears. To Griffyn's surprise, it worked like a charm. The spears penetrated the Dwellers and halted their charge as confusion overtook them.

"Charge!" A second order made by Wilson as the soldiers that stood behind the long spears charged and butchered the retreating Dwellers, who began to panic.

This is how you use tactics to destroy an unprepared opponent. Griffyn would make sure to etch this into his memory. The skills of a great tactician, like Wilson, did the impossible. All he had to do was to wait for them to catch up.

# CHAPTER 9

## *Lord*

Drenched in sweat, Griffyn jumped.

"You were a fool."

Those fading words were the last he heard as his eyes shot open. "Griffyn!" It was Wilson who held the boy. "Why is it always the brave ones that kill us all?" he said as he got up.

"What happened to Leah?"

"She'll be well," he said as he sighed. "She needs to rest. You too."

"No, we don't have time." Griffyn mumbled despite his state. He got up. "We must leave here right now."

Wilson stopped. "What did you say?"

"We can't remain here."

"What do you suggest we do?"

"We go to the Citadel."

"This is why you are a boy, and a fool at that as well," Wilson said as he turned his back on him and started to walk away. Griffyn's veins popped as his brows narrowed.

"And what would experience dictate in such a position?" he challenged as he turned his palms into fists.

"You would drive at the heart of the enemy, deeper, instead of retreating to a safer position. You give away not only any hope of survival, but when there is such a difference in power, you do not take them on in open battle." Wilson explained.

"And your solution?"

"Draw the battle out. Wear them out, delay as much as possible—"

"The more you delay, the stronger the enemy gets."

"But so do we, Griffyn, so do we."

"This is madness, Wilson," Griffyn intercepted. "Look, I don't know why, but I think that there's—"

"Enough!" Wilson interrupted.

"Swallow your damn pride, Wilson. I get what you're going through, but this is nonsense!" Griffyn yelled.

"Wait!" Wilson shouted. "Do you hear that?"

The entire place laid silent. It was subtle, but when Griffyn's gaze fell upon a single leaf on the ground, he was certain of it. The leaf shifted left and then right.

"Footsteps," Griffyn said.

Wilson narrowed his brows. "A lot of them. This is an army," he said before he sighed. "Prepare for battle!" he gave the command. Almost instantly, soldiers rushed towards the front and formed a wall of shields.

Griffyn took a step closer to Wilson.

"Don't press me again, boy," Wilson threatened.

Griffyn frowned. Though he knew that this wasn't the time. "What are we even facing?" he asked.

"I haven't a clue. Demons, bandits..." he took a breath, "...Gods?" he added as sweat began to form on his forehead. If there was anything any battle commander feared the most it was the unknown. Lack of information and preparation played a significant role in the downfall of many heroes, but Wilson would not have his now.

Griffyn's frown turned as his brows touched and his nose flared. He resented Wilson's decision, but would fight with him right now and right here to see that he survives. He's still a good man. And as far as I know, we are short of that nowadays, he thought as he drew the Masamune.

A few thuds echoed on the ground before everything halted. If there was one thing people hated before a battle it was the sound of silence. Nothing good ever came from it.

"What's happening?" a soldier asked.

A loud horn played. It was of a different tone then the ones that Wilson used, but Griffyn felt it familiar. The silence grew, but soon afterwards, the footsteps stopped.

There were two men riding on brown horses. One of them held a white flag.

"I don't get it, they're surrendering?" Griffyn asked.

Wilson shook his head. "They're asking for an audience."

"But I thought—"

"The sooner you realize you aren't in a fairy tale, the better, kid."

Griffyn scratched the top of his head and followed Wilson.

"Where do you think you're going?"

"Look, you're obviously not getting rid of me anytime soon, so just let me come."

Wilson took a deep breath. "Only if you keep your mouth shut," he said as he stopped. He grabbed Griffyn and pulled him closer. "Can you do that?"

Griffyn nodded as he jumped up on the horse brought by a soldier for their captain. "She's a beauty," Griffyn said.

"That she is," Wilson agreed as he got up as well. "We actually found it near the city walls shortly after you came."

Griffyn's eyes widened. "Oh..." he mumbled as he

took Wilson's hand, and the two neared the passing horsemen. The closer they got, the better Griffyn could make the details of one of them. Gruntled, and in his forties, he didn't have a pleasant aura. His beard was clipped and he had a pointy nose and short curly brown hair. He wore a plate armor and resting on the breastplate was a mark Griffyn knew too well.

"Of the light by the light," the man said as he dismounted and took a few steps closer. "The name's Kaven. A general in the army of light. Who do I have the pleasure of speaking to?"

"Captain Wilson Harlet, and I will pretend I did not hear you just now address your status to an official Captain of the Royal Army. Now, how may I help you?"

"It is customary to get off your horse when you speak to someone, Captain," Kaven said as he spread his arms apart. "Will you not offer me such courtesy?"

"Spare me the bravado, and tell me why you are here."

"We heard a noise, Captain," Kaven said as his eyes narrowed. "It is only normal for one to worry about the status of the world around them, wouldn't you say?"

"Don't be coy with me, traitor. State your desire, or I'll have you executed right where you are."

"Give it time, sir. Soon there will be no Royal Army for you to belong to," Kaven said as he kept his gaze fixed on Wilson. "But alas, I digress," he paused. "The noise sounded like what comes out of our Commander's sword.

You wouldn't know where he would be, would you?"

"Wait!" Griffyn said as he tried to get off the horse, but Wilson laid an elbow to his side.

"Who goes there?" Kaven said as he shifted his head trying to catch a glimpse of Griffyn.

"No one of your concern. Return to where you were. Honor dictates that I put you to the sword right now, but unfortunately there are customs that I cannot abandon, lest I turn into one of you," As he was about to turn, Griffyn jumped down the horse. "You idiot!" Wilson shouted.

"If you're who I think you are, then you know Natasha? And Rory? Tatiana and Dale..."

Kaven took a step back. "Have we met before, young boy?"

"No, but—"

"That sword you hold, it is not yours. You will give it back, thief!" the other soldier that was with Kaven exclaimed before he drew his sword and pointed it at Griffyn.

"Put down your sword, you halfwit," Kaven said as he slapped the sword aside and eyed the soldier down.

"But, General, there is no mistaking it—"

"Do you honestly believe a boy could disarm the Commander?" Kaven shot the soldier down with a gaze. "Perhaps he bested him, hm? If that boy has the Commander's sword, then there is only one possibility. He received it from him personally."

Griffyn stared at them, his tongue at the back of his mouth, unable to form the most basic of words.

"Run back to where you came from, and I will do the same," Wilson said as he strolled up slowly and grabbed Griffyn.

"I'm afraid I can't let you do that now," Kaven said as he came forward. "For the good of our kind..." he began as his voice trembled. "Because if that boy holds that sword, and if the Commander truly did pass it to him...then there is only one reality. One concept that remains; the Commander is dead."

Wilson froze. As if he was compelled to do so, his pupils dilated as he heard those words. Perhaps there were some truths hidden between the lies that the empire fed about him, but none can deny how terribly fearsome he was, he thought to himself.

"Wilson," Griffyn whispered as he gently pushed him aside and took a few steps towards Kaven. "He was the bravest man I knew."

Those words sent a shiver down Kaven's spine and forced him to the ground, as if his legs could not bear the weight that burdened him.

"You lie! The Commander would never fall to scum like you!" the other man shouted.

"Still your tongue," Kaven ordered. "You need to come with us. If the Commander believed in you, then so shall we."

"That is not the answer," Griffyn replied. "He fought them bravely, but even he was no match for them. Not all of them."

"How many were there?"

"Two."

Kaven let out a laugh. "I do not know what to believe in anymore... but if all has gone downhill, then it is only right to do something that would befit the fate that fell upon us," Kaven finally stood up. "You need to come with us."

"Out of the question," Wilson said as he unsheathed his sword. "This boy is the key to our salvation. I would die before I hand him to traitors."

"It was your King who betrayed you, not them," Griffyn shouted as he turned his face towards him. "Through his actions, he ordained divine war against all of us, yet you still brand them as traitors? Them? The only ones who are fighting to save mankind from whatever fate the Gods have deemed just?"

"What do you expect me to do?" Wilson's hands began to shake.

"It is time, Wilson, to place your trust in me, as I did you. There are things at play, and I think I am the only one who can stop all of this."

Kaven took a few steps. "What would you do?" he

looked at Griffyn.

"I'd join hands," Griffyn looked at Kaven. "His soldiers are battle hardened. And if we both join hands, then perhaps we can salvage something, anything."

"Our armies are sworn to the Red Hand. They will not follow anyone. Only the Second may decide what's next for us. And that is precisely why I want you to come with us. If Wilson would like to follow, then I don't mind, but know that in doing so, we go towards Fort Eldren, which is besieged."

"Besieged by what?" Wilson asked. "Few even are aware of that name."

"I've not the faintest idea. But I believe it to be those-"

"Dwellers, it has to be," Griffyn interrupted. He scratched his lower chin, and turned around to face Wilson. "We need them, you know that, right?"

Wilson shook his head. "We are not fighting the war on their behalf."

"Maybe that is the problem. What need would the world have of the Red Hand had you done your job and protected us?" Kaven shot at him.

Wilson unsheathed his sword and pointed it at him. "I would demand you back up those words, but I'm afraid I haven't the time for this nonsense."

"Will you two stop behaving like children?" Griffyn said as he stepped between them. "The Red Hand is dead.

The King is dead. It is up to us, the survivors, to make best of a bad situation. Can you not feel them wreathing in agony? Do you not hear the cries of the helpless?"

Wilson hesitated, but lowered his sword. Kaven turned his back. "Boy," Kaven shouted before he started walking again. "The decision you must make is your own. When you realize that these washed up army dogs are no good, come and find us at the Fort," he muttered. Kaven took a few steps, but then turned his head just enough to eye Griffyn down. "And whatever you do, don't lose that sword."

Wilson tried to speak, but the words wouldn't come out. Are they right? Doubt seemed to dwell within him. Normally, he would respond with something witty. However, he couldn't shake off the feeling that he got from Griffyn. A boy had become wiser than him, an experienced Captain who fought many wars and had prevailed.

Griffyn gently touched Wilson's shoulder. His pupils dilated, and for a moment, they turned blue before returning to normal. "The answer is not might... do you hear the silence that severs the heart? Do you not see that we are the darkness that is fighting the light this time? There are no traitors anymore; they have all perished."

As both of them turned, Kaven was well on his way back towards where he came from. His steps were heavy, but they remained solid, nonetheless. "Kaven!" Griffyn cried.

Kaven stopped and turned to face him.

# TITANLORD

"Of the light, by the light," the words left Griffyn's lips of their own accord. He had heard them repeatedly uttered by Natasha and even Tatiana before.

The words felt like knives that pierced Kaven's heart. He covered his face for a second and smiled. "Perhaps not all hope is lost," Kaven said as he continued on his path.

# CHAPTER 10

## *Purpose*

A spark flew towards Griffyn as he strolled back towards their camp near the lake accompanied by Wilson. None of them spoke a single word until they made it past the back ends and reached the center where Wilson's tent had been waiting.

Wilson got off the horse. "I have some matters to attend to, care to join me?" he asked.

"I would rather speak with the troops," Griffyn replied.

Wilson paused before entering the tent. "Send her my regards," he said as he disappeared inside.

"Asshole..." Griffyn mumbled as he turned around. He almost didn't recognize the camp; in a matter of hours everything was set up. There were military tents on the

# TITANLORD

outskirts, and anything that didn't involve fighting resided more towards the center. It was more of a moving city than a camp.

Griffyn scanned his surrounding but couldn't find any hints of Leah's whereabouts. He spent a good amount of time looking for her, but finally yielded and asked one of the soldiers around camp.

"Good day, soldier!" he said.

"Good day, sir," the soldier replied.

"Where's Leah Pilthiel, the one injured taken?" he asked.

"She is staying in the medic's tent. Should be the one right next to the Captain's, sir."

"Ah, thank you," he replied as he retraced his steps. *He could've told me where she was instead of acting like a child, again* he thought to himself. He reached the medic's tent in no time and entered.

He blocked his nose with his hand. "Ah! What the hell is that!" he shouted. There were many beds, some were empty while others were not. Though most of them were covered with a sheet, it didn't do much for the smell.

"Not so loud," an older man replied, coming towards him. "Apologies, it is the smell of alcohol and Angel Tears."

"Angel tears? I've never heard of that before."

"I'm not surprised. It's as rare an ingredient as they

come," the medic said as he turned around. "So long as you're here, boy, mind if you fetch an old man a drink?"

"A drink? Shouldn't you be tending to Leah instead?"

"Oh, apologies, it's my mistake. You did mention that you didn't know what Angel Tears were," the medic said before he turned around yet again and faced Griffyn. "See it's used to dwell deep within-" he stopped as Griffyn's face went hollow.

"Where is she," Griffyn repeated the words faster than he thought them. Not again, he thought to himself as he hastened towards the bed he saw earlier.

"Boy, don't do that. I am sorry, I didn't know, lest I—" the medic rushed towards Griffyn and grabbed his shoulder. "I said don't..."

"Leave me be," Griffyn shouted at the medic. His eyes pulsed. The medic let go of him and exited the tent. It happened again, he thought to himself before turning his attention to the bed. He slowly revealed the body that rested beneath the sheets.

He grabbed Leah's hand. It was cold, yet something was different than when he held it normally. He used her hand to cover his face.

"I am so sorry," he said as his tone broke. His brows narrowed and his breath became labored. "God dammit... What use am I if the only purpose to my existence is to watch those around me perish by those who claim superiority over me..." he lifted his head and shouted from the

# TITANLORD

top of his lungs.

"Am I not the God Child? Am I not supposed to be supreme and powerful! Then how the fuck do you explain this? All of this!" he paused as he tried to catch his breath. "God damn you, Veda! May the curse of the Creator fall upon you for what you have made me live!" he stopped, the sound of his voice growing weaker. There was a ruckus outside the tent suddenly.

He could hear soldiers shouting and calling for Wilson to attend to the boy who had delivered miracle after miracle.

"No, I refuse," Griffyn shook his head. "I am drawing the line right here and right now," Griffyn. "Bring them back. All of them. Leah, Cory... Bring all of them back. Roriana, Benjen and Vendel. You fucking bastard, do you hear me? Or I will walk to Nepherin and present him my head. Right this moment."

He closed his eyes shut, and then opened them. He could see the soldiers rushing towards him, yet everything was frozen. It was as if life had paused itself. A being manifested in front of him.

"You dishonor yourself," the being said as it levitated in the air. His pupils were dark blue.

"The dishonor is yours, King of Titans." Griffyn said as his brows narrowed.

"You think this a joke?"

"Perhaps," Griffyn let out a laugh. "What would you

call all of this? How can you expect someone to go through such tragedies, and yet remain whole?" Griffyn fell to his knees. "I can't do this, Veda, I am not strong enough."

"And now you insult Pollus and all those who died so you could live."

"You fucking twat... do you think I don't see what you're doing? You called me the God Child, well, can the God Child bring back the dead?"

"Death is final. By rule of the Architect."

"That is not a no. I'm not kidding. I can't do this, not alone, I need company and those who would keep me sane. Roriana, Benjen and Vendel, Leah too... the planet has better odds with them."

"You negotiate with the wrong being."

Griffyn smirked. "Maybe you're right, maybe I should be talking to a real God."

Veda shook his head as he sighed. "There are matters in this world that will remain unknown, even to those who bear the Voice. You lack motivation, and even now in your darkest moments, you do not seek the return of the dead, but rather, you desire the will to keep fighting. Yet that is something that should be inherently yours."

"I am not strong enough. What don't you fucking get?"

"You're not? Then perhaps I made a mistake? Perhaps Benjen and Pollus mistook you for someone you're not. Is that your argument?"

# TITANLORD

"You said it yourself; you're not perfect beings, unlike the new Children of the Creator."

"Snarky." Veda said as he smiled and lowered his head. He lifted it and walked closer towards Griffyn. "Leah is dead because you couldn't control your power. Roriana is dead because she didn't listen to me when I told her never to look back. Benjen was not strong enough, that is all. Now, will you grow up and start behaving like a Titanlord?"

The words sunk into the back of Griffyn's mind. He vaguely remembered those exact words that Veda uttered when he was fighting Nepherin, when Rory and him were running away. 'No matter what you do, don't look back.' There was no mistaking it. Veda had warned them. "You think this a game?" Griffyn huffed.

"There's a winner and a loser. That's a game, isn't it?" Veda said as he extended his hand. "I cannot promise you anything, Griffyn, but know that you will be central to humanity's salvation."

"I am not strong enough, Veda. Two Titan powers aren't enough," he said.

"And who said there were only two Titans?"

"Veda, Pollus, and Magnus..." Griffyn recited as he tilted his head towards him. "Are you saying there are more?"

Veda sighed. "That statement exists only because of a religion devoted to us. Yes, along with myself, Pollus and

Magnus, there are others, but us three were the most prominent."

"Where can I find them?"

"I do not know," Veda said as his narrowed. "We are your weapons, Titanlord. You will rise and be the light that surpasses the darkness."

Griffyn lowered his head. "I get it. It's like I'm asking for a miracle in a fight that the Creator has left us with..."

"Know that every step you take, others are watching from above. So, do not dishonor them again. Give them a sight to behold. Show them that when darkness falls, your light will shine the brightest," Veda took a pause. "Do you understand what I am saying, Titanlord?"

Griffyn finally took his hand. "I do," he stood up and wiped his tears away with his shirt. "Very well. I am ready," he said as he kept staring at Veda.

"Ready for what?" Veda asked.

"Undo...this," he said as he looked towards his surroundings. "That," he pointed towards a soldier that seemed frozen in time.

Veda smiled. "I didn't cause this, you did."

Griffyn's eyes widened as he began to blink faster. In an instant, everything returned to normal. Yet, something seemed lighter, the soldiers fell to their knees. Griffyn's brows rose.

"What's going on?" Wilson barked as he entered the

# TITANLORD

tent and grabbed one soldier after another until his eyes fell upon Griffyn. His pupils dilated. "What...what's going on?" he mumbled.

Griffyn looked at his hands. They were glowing. There were three colors emitting from him as if a light had been lit: blue, orange and purple. He turned around and saw Leah's lifeless body levitating in the air.

It took him a moment, but he noticed the other bodies were floating in the air as well. Something was going on, and it was not the Titan Power doing it, of that he was certain.

"No," he said out loud. "There are some things in life that one can only accept. Now I know," he took a pause. "Now I know," he repeated.

The bodies fell onto their beds yet again. Griffyn smiled gently as he saw the soldier prostrating before him. Wilson was the only one who stood still. Though his legs were shaking, unable to decipher the lights coming from him.

"Men of the North," Griffyn addressed them gently. "If I ever desire to be worshiped, I shall let you know," he said as he looked into their eyes. "Rise."

# CHAPTER 11

## *City of Thieves*

**H**idden deep within the mountains, overlooking Robrin's Pass, laid a city that those who knew existed avoided. Ospis, a city that had no military presence, and the Crown did not recognize it. Its location was a prime defensive stronghold that none even dared venture to with an army.

The city was built atop a hill surrounded by a deep drench and shouldered by tall mountains. Many had argued that the structure was far too advanced to be a cause of nature, but those legends have all simmered down. Within the outskirts, laid the city's militia, which numbered a few thousands.

History books were not kind to them, but whenever a King or a bandit group attempted to lay siege to it, they were met with a crushing defeat. 'A few dozen can hold out an army,' or so it is spoken.

It was afternoon. The sun basked in all its glory and casted shadows upon two dozen men and women who stood still, as silent as the grave. They tried not to gaze nor shift their attention when the doors to the barracks barged open.

In walked a man who dressed in light brown attire. He was bold, his skin tone closer to brown than white. He was at least six feet tall and had broad shoulders. Darting grey eyes kept shifting upon his surroundings as he meticulosity approached the crowd that had gathered.

"Recruits," he shouted, and they all stomped their feet. "I've been told that you lot have volunteered to play safe keepers to the safest city in mankind's history."

A grin slowly shaped on his face. "I can't help but wonder why...is it bravery? Or plain idiocy? I suppose there's one way to find out," he added as he kept walking parallel to them.

"You," he stopped. "Come forth," his tone brooked no argument. He kept his gaze upon the man that obeyed.

"Sir."

"What is your name?"

"Donovan Skully, sir."

"And what is it you do, Skully?"

"I was a farmer, sir."

"And what did you use to farm?"

"Cucumbers, apples and corn, sir."

"And why is it that you decided to cast all that out and join us in this shithole?"

"The world is in chaos, sir...I've a daughter I want to keep safe."

"And who will keep them safe when you shit your life away?" he smirked at him. "Back in line," he demanded and moved on towards another.

"You, step forth," he signaled a man with his finger.

"Sir."

"And what did you use to be before coming here?"

"Military, sir."

"Oh, royalty!" The man gasped. "How did you end up here?"

"After the Capital fell, a few soldiers were sent defending the outskirt villages, sir."

"And you left your post and ran all the way here, is that right? Sir?" the man mimicked.

"I disagree with you, sir."

"Oh, is that right?"

"That's right, sir. Retreating to fight another battle is a winning strategy, sir."

The man paused for a moment, and then burst into laughter. The people gathered didn't know what to make of it. Confusion spread amongst them. "You disagree with me?" he said as he stepped closer towards him.

"Let me tell you something, son," He grabbed the man from his shirt and pulled him closer. He locked his eyes with his. "Whatever strategy you think you know means absolute shit here, do you hear me?"

"I hear you, sir," the soldier shot back at him.

"In war, there is only the strength to move forward. All of your captain cunts will have you running like the shits you are, but they will never tell you the truth; strategy means shit if those following it are worthless cunts like you."

Silence. His words rang true in everyone's mind. Whatever went on in the Capital had echoed across the entire continent, but not one of them could doubt how true his words felt.

"Get back in fucking line," he broke the silence, and the soldier backed away.

"I know what you lot are thinking. And you're probably right. We don't know what the fuck is going on, but there is one thing for certain; Ospis has always fended off any form of attack, whatever it may be," he said before he cleared his throat. "Do you think it is because those who tried didn't try hard enough?"

As he was talking, a tall man approached. He wore a broad jacket that hung on his shoulders loosely. His hair was blonde. He stepped closer and placed his hand on the man's shoulder. "Kog?"

"I want you to remember one thing and one thing only; the world owes you shit. It was here first. None of you retain the rights nor the titles that you once did before you stepped inside these walls. You will all train, and train hard. But what merit you have will depend on your skill and hard work alone."

He took a good look at the men. "Is that clear?" he demanded, and they all nodded in unison. "Dismissed!" he barked and all of them moved in the opposite direction.

Kog turned around and faced the tall man. "Came to enjoy the show? Did you miss my lectures?"

"Not now, Kog. You are being summoned."

"Good," he said as he turned around and started moving towards the door. "Be a good boy and tell them to go fuck themselves, will you?" he spat as he squeezed the handle.

"Kog!" the man shouted at him. Kog eased his grip on the handle.

"What?"

The man swallowed and took a sigh. "There's a horde."

Kog let go of the handle and turned around yet again. "A what now?" he asked as he took a few steps forward.

"A horde... of things... we don't know what, or how they got here, but it is a horde nonetheless," the man added.

"What a wise man you are. Explaining what a fucking

horde is," Kog mocked. "What are they? Army, bandits? Or those damn things?"

"I believe they are what you refer to as damn things."

Kog placed one hand on his chin and another on his head. "Then we're royally fucked it seems."

"Dammit, Kog, just come to the meeting."

"Fuck that," Kog said as he began walking towards the walls. "Ring that fucking bell as loud as you can, and call in the Militia. I have work to do."

# CHAPTER 12

## *Letters in Blood*

Energetic, Griffyn smiled from ear to ear. He was on a horse, riding slowly. He had never ridden a horse before, not by himself. Riled dust surrounded the army's march as he was accompanied by Wilson. He would look at his surroundings every time he had a chance. That's quite a scene, he thought to himself.

"Breathtaking, isn't it?" Wilson said.

"I'll say that again..." Griffyn responded as he glanced towards Wilson. He tightened his grip on the reigns.

"Don't do that," Wilson cried. "You'll either scare the horse or have it sprint and knock you away."

"I'd do that just by changing the way I hold the reigns?"

"Horses are intelligent. They are far more noble than most men," Wilson said as a smile crept onto his lips. "I enjoy their company."

"Wilson," Griffyn shook his head. "That's just because you don't have any friends."

A few of the soldiers marching along with them tried to hold their laughter. It wasn't often that someone would speak to their Captain this way.

"Oh, shut up and keep at it," Wilson cried to his surroundings. "I take comfort in the fact that I place my duty beyond anything else. A thing that comes with experience—"

"Did it ever occur to you why no one likes talking to you?" Griffyn cut him off. "Just listen to yourself..."

"You're telling me to have fun? When the world has gone to shit?"

"That is exactly why you should have as much fun as you can," Griffyn said as he paused. "The world is cruel, but you yourself shouldn't reflect a reality that you aim to change."

"You think words can change the world, young man?"

Griffyn shook his head. "I'm saying that in order to rebel against a cruel world, one must not become cruel themselves."

Wilson smirked. "Wise. Almost as wise as my grandmother."

"I'm sure she's a lovely lady."

"She's dead. We're here." Wilson said as he raised his hand for all to see. The command echoed as his generals replicated the act and brought the entire army to a halt. "I hope I don't regret this," Wilson added.

"Yeah, so do I," Griffyn agreed as he rode a bit further and turned around to face the army.

He struggled for a moment to fully halt the horse. "Stop, hey, stop!" he shouted as the horse kept moving.

Wilson stared at him and covered his face as he sighed. "Pull the reigns, idiot." He shouted.

"What do you think I'm doing!"

"Just don't move. Pull it hard, and place booth your feet at its stomach."

Griffyn did as Wilson said, and the horse came to a stop. "Goodness...everyone at Palleria said this was the easiest thing for a child to do."

"It is clear then that you in fact cannot hide behind that excuse. You're not a child; just an idiot," Wilson said as he strolled up next to him.

"Funny," Griffyn said as he took a deep breath.

"You don't have to do this," Wilson said as he gazed into his eyes. "We can go somewhere else."

"And do what?" Griffyn asked as he turned and yanked on the reigns. "You promised you'd let me try, remember!" he shouted as he moved towards the gates of Wynne.

# TITANLORD

The Red Hand's banners flew across it, and Griffyn knew one thing for certain; either they believe him that the Red Hand offered him his sword and sacrificed himself, or that he simply looted his corpse.

Well, towards bigger things, he thought and stopped at the gate. "Hello?" he shouted.

"Who goes there?" A soldier cried back.

"My name is Griffyn Haikrou. I am here to talk with Kaven Holt. Please inform him of my arrival at once."

There was silence. Griffyn squinted to see a discussion amongst the soldiers. Someone then stepped from atop the walls. A familiar face.

"You arrive at the head of the Royal army? Why then would we open the doors and welcome you with open arms?" Said a man.

"Dale? Is that you?" Griffyn shouted.

"Go back the way you came, little lord." Dale replied, and then turned his back. He tilted enough to see Griffyn from the corner of his eye. "We have more pressing concerns here."

"More important than the fate of your Commander?" Griffyn shot back at him.

Dale paused for a while, but then resumed as if he heard nothing. What the hell is wrong with him? Griffyn stepped closer. "I want to talk to Tatiana," he shouted. "Do you hear me?"

Griffyn kept eyeing Dale. What he said seemed to work as Dale turned back and came closer to the edge atop the wall. He borrowed a bow, loaded it with an arrow, and shot at Griffyn.

The arrow dove down towards Griffyn, gravity seeming to work against him, as the arrow shot at top speed and was almost invisible. Griffyn jumped to the right to avoid it, yet the arrow just barely grazed his left cheek, knocking him off the horse. Blood came dripping down.

He swiped the blood away. "Bastard!" he shouted.

"Griffyn!" Wilson shouted as he rushed towards him. He offered his hand as he neared. "Grab my hand!"

Griffyn grabbed it, and Wilson lifted him atop his horse. "You idiot, what were you thinking?"

"Wait, don't go back! If you go back, then it means a war-"

"Are you trying to get yourself killed? There is no talking between us and them after this, he's made sure of that."

"That's just the thing, I don't think Kaven knows of this. Dale has always been one to be moved by emotions and reckless judgment."

"More for you to think about," Wilson said as he went behind the lines. "Prepare for battle!" he cried, and the soldiers struck their shields on the ground.

"Shit," Griffyn cursed.

"Is that it? Is that all you have to say?" Wilson spat.

# TITANLORD

"Leave me alone, I'm trying to think."

"Well, do it fast, lest the battle starts," Wilson said as they turned their gaze to the walls of Wynne. Archers had filled their positions, and the bell rang so loud that it reached them outside.

"He is alone in this, he must be."

"What makes you say that, huh? Because a while ago you were their prisoner?"

"You were there when we spoke to Kaven. I think news of the Red Hand's fate has already spread, and it must've caused a dispute amongst them."

"Griffyn, I've listened to you, out of respect for what you said in that meeting, and I think there is strategic value in fortifying ourselves somewhere that overlooks the Shred, but now, you must listen to me."

"Well, how are you going to respond then?"

"A siege."

"A siege?"

"We can run a supply line of water and send soldiers to gather provisions. We can outlast them," Wilson explained.

"Provided they're not stocked on the same."

"They've just taken this village. It's just a shame that it's Wynne. Everyone knows that they aspire to be recognized as more. That's why they've built fortifications to try and pass for a city," Wilson said as he dismounted from the horse and took a few steps forward. Griffyn followed suit.

"Does that even work?"

"Provided they add value to the Crown and are loyal, I don't see why not," Wilson scratched his lower chin.

"I'm not so sure of anything anymore," Griffyn said as he scratched the back of his head. "I think that if we-"

Griffyn halted. He felt a chill run down his spine. He gasped. Wilson came to him. "What's wrong?" he asked as he grabbed him. "Griffyn!"

Find the Teetans to the south. Griffyn heard a voice speak to him. "Did you hear that?" he asked Wilson as he pushed him aside. He staggered and fell to his knees.

"Medic!" Wilson cried at his surroundings.

Soldiers raced around to adhere to Wilson's request, but Griffyn waved with his hand. "I'm fine, I think I just...heard the Voice."

Wilson's brows narrowed. "What did it say this time?"

"'Find the Teetans in the south.' Not sure—"

"Teetans?" Wilson interrupted as he leaned closer. "Are you sure it said find the Teetans?"

"Yeah, I think I heard about them before."

"They're a cult, Griffyn."

"They worship the Voice Titan." Griffyn clarified.

"They worship many Titans. Veda, Pollus, and other

damned names from fairy books spoken in whispers at night to make children sleep."

Griffyn locked eyes with him. "So, what am I then? A story?" he said as he took a pause and looked around. "I have to go."

Wilson squinted his eyes and veins popped out on his forehead. "I truly don't understand what most of this means, but you will not go."

"Wilson..." Griffyn mumbled.

"I'll send a search party to the south and look for them. You're too important to run errands now, Griffyn."

"And if they find them?"

"Only then do you ride towards them," Wilson extended a hand and looked Griffyn in the eye.

Griffyn pondered for a moment and shook his hand.

"Soldier," Wilson shouted, and one of them came rushing in.

"Captain," he said as he stomped the ground.

"Prepare a search party and ride south. Should you see any sign of Teetans, you are to report back immediately. Do you understand?" Wilson asked.

"Yes, Captain." The soldier turned around.

"Wait," Griffyn shouted. "What if they run into them?" he said as he glanced towards Wilson.

Wilson shook his head and kept his gaze on the soldier. "If you find them, tell them that our lovely friend who has deep brown eyes, that sometimes turn blue, would like to have a word."

The soldier nodded and went straight away.

"Really?"

Wilson turned around and looked at Griffyn. "What?" he waved his hands. "I have to make this fun for me too."

Griffyn shook his head. "I just hope he doesn't actually say that to the fanatics..."

# CHAPTER 13

## *The Grand Design*
## *(Sometime in the future)*

**S**ilence gloomed in Hollow Land. Ceris was jogging against the dust that riled up from his movement. He was panting, with only one thing clear in his mind. He reached the top of the hill that oversaw nearly all the visible points in Hollow Land and paused when he reached Colossal.

He was perfectly still. Not a movement, not a breath, or any sign that indicated his consciousness. It was clear; Colossal had gone into slumber. Yet Ceris stood before him, panting heavily and calling his name. "Colossal... I know you've seen it too..."

Still, Colossal didn't seem to respond in the least bit. Ceris knew that was meant to happen. It was meant to be.

For some odd reason that he didn't understand, Colossal was destined to go into a slumber and awake only when time dictated as such.

Yet there was a fire in his eyes. Something that he'd seen that would come to be, something unimaginable that would turn the tide of the war at their hands. As patterns were beginning to change, and signs foretelling of a fate far worse than death, he would do the unthinkable; raise Colossal from his slumber at all costs.

"If the Creator has willed what I have just seen, he wouldn't have shown it to me, Colossal...You must rise! This shadow cannot be cast, or all of light as we know it will perish." He said as his voice broke down. Tears began running down his cheeks.

"Colossal... I beg of you... There won't be enough time to save them," he pleaded a final time as he fell to his knees. He drove his hands into the dirt below him and placed his forehead on the ground. "Then why show this to me! If after everything that we endured and saw come to pass, why show me the end if the only one capable to stop it lays in a deep slumber! Why!"

Ceris felt a beckoning. A tingle that played gently within his heart. He stopped, and slowly tilted his head up towards Colossal. His eyes were wide open.

"Colossal..." he whispered.

"On your feet, old man," Colossal commanded.

"You're awake..." Ceris could only see his back. "Does

# TITANLORD

that mean-"

"I've seen it too," he said, and silence stalked them for but a moment. For whatever reason, Ceris had pulled him out of it. "It's at risk. The Grand Design."

"I had no other choice Colossal... forgive me," Ceris said as his eyes hollowed out. "I know what this will do to you... but for the first time in ages, I didn't know what else-"

Colossal turned and gazed into his eyes. "You've done the right thing. The balance is tipped, but then again..." Colossal paused, cocked his hand in his pocket and took out an amulet. He balled his hand into a fist.

He then squeezed tightly. The amulet burst in his hand.

"Now, the time is ripe."

# CHAPTER 14

## *Defiance*

Somber was the color of the sky. Griffyn awoke from his slumber and made his way outside the tent. He covered his eyes as the light dazzled against the shadows. A light so bright that sparked his naturally gray eyes.

"You're awake, good." Wilson said as he gave a letter to a soldier and nodded him away. "Follow me," he commanded as both of them walked towards the village.

"It's been a fortnight, and we still haven't heard anything from the search party. I should go and check it out."

"Have faith, Griffyn. So far we don't know when they'll make their next move."

"Maybe there's a dispute amongst them," Griffyn said as he scratched his lower chin.

# TITANLORD

"What I want to know is why that damn voice doesn't tell us the way to victory already," Wilson said, and as he finished a soldier came rushing up to them. "Captain! There's unusual activity on the walls!"

Griffyn looked at Wilson. Their gazes caught up with the walls of Wynne. "I think it's safe to call this a city now."

The gates were being opened for some reason. "Why would they do that?" Griffyn asked.

"It's bait. They think we'll try to rush inside only to be slaughtered by arrows."

"I think you mean fire arrows," Griffyn said as he swallowed. He could almost feel his heart in his throat, beating so loud as if a drum were playing.

There was a quiver next to each archer. Torches were being lit. Something was coming. Wilson and Griffyn both knew it.

"Wilson," Griffyn's voice shook. "Tell me how to defeat these things," he pleaded.

Wilson kept his gaze fixed on the wall. "You don't," he said with a sigh. "The damage those damn things cause is too much for any army."

Griffyn swallowed yet again. "What if we get too close? They wouldn't fire on their own soldiers."

"I suppose that's exactly what they're counting on. Thus, the opened fucking door."

"What do you mean?"

"They're threatening us," Wilson's gaze didn't shift. "Either retreat and break the siege, or charge in and try to beat the arrows."

Griffyn's mouth opened wide. "That's... genius..."

"Yeah," Wilson wasn't amused.

"But Dale isn't smart enough to come up with this."

Wilson's head shifted towards Griffyn. "Explain."

"I spent a lot of time with Dale. Granted, he never struck me as a bright fellow, but this kind of tactic? I'd expect from Ben. Not from Dale."

Wilson's face lit up as a thin smile formed on his lips. "You know why everyone feared the Red Hand?"

"Why?"

"Because the moment he would make a single move, it would be too late to stop him. Because chances are, he had already seen the end." Wilson turned his focus back on the arrows. "This, right here, isn't his work because they need us to make the first move."

"How do you know so much about him?" Griffyn asked.

"I fought him once. It was the opposite; he was the one laying siege to us. Took months to actually end the battle."

"How bad did you lose?"

Wilson's brows narrowed as he turned. "Lose is an understatement," he said as his brows deepened. "I'll tell you about it one day, if we survive."

Griffyn gazed at him.

"Retr-"

"Hold on!" Griffyn interrupted. "Don't give the order just yet," he added as he pointed towards the walls again. "Does that mean they surrender?" he asked.

Wilson turned around and stared at a bright white flag being swung by one of the soldiers. A carriage seemed to appear from inside the gate.

"They're requesting an audience," Wilson sighed.

"With who? Me?" Griffyn asked.

Wilson smirked as he grabbed Griffyn by the chest. "Listen, boy, I've grown accustomed to your idiocy, and while I admit there's something about you that pulls one to serve, I am still Captain of this regiment. Is that clear?"

"I didn't mean anything by it."

"Follow me," Wilson said as he got on the horse and extended a hand. Griffyn tilted his head for a moment, and through the sun setting, he could almost see Wilson's eyes flare up with the same light as the sun. He paused for a moment.

"Well?" Wilson asked.

Griffyn smiled and took his hand yet again as they rode towards the carriage that came to meet them.

"What was that just now?" Wilson wondered

"Maybe I'm coming to terms that I don't actually hate you, but rather respect the way you lead."

Wilson gawked. His brows narrowed, but then he smiled. "It is a burden, one that only the cursed one's bear."

"Why do you say that?"

"One day you'll understand," Wilson said as he pulled the reigns, halting in front of the carriage. "Do you recognize him?"

Griffyn squinted his eyes long enough to make out some details. "That's him. Stupid Dale," he said as he stepped down and walked towards him.

Wilson quickly followed him. "Hey, hey!" he said as he pulled Griffyn. "Let me go. I have matters to discuss with him."

"Don't do anything rash, okay? If there's any moment for you to stop behaving like a child, it's now."

Griffyn locked gazes with Wilson and nodded. For brief moment, Griffyn's pupil flashed orange. Wilson staggered and stepped back.

Griffyn shifted his eyes towards Dale, and walked slowly. Wilson followed in pursuit. "You need to explain yourselves right now."

Dale took a hard look at him. "By what right do you speak to me, you stupid little idiot?"

Griffyn pulled the Masamune and struck it on the

# TITANLORD

ground. The dust riled up and reached Dale's chin. His eyes dilated and his brows shot up.

"Test me again. Go ahead, I'll wait," Griffyn said as he locked his gaze with Dale's.

"Put away the sword, Griffyn," said a man sat next to Dale. "If we are to have a proper conversation, waving that sword might provoke some all too fresh wounds."

"That's just the thing," Griffyn shook his head. "You are followers of his. I was there when he challenged the Gods single-handedly and bought me enough time to escape," Griffyn paused to take a deep breath. "You all claim that you are followers of the Red Hand, but the way I see you—"

"We're what? Go on! Say it!" Dale shouted.

"You're lost," Griffyn lowered his voice. "Why did you sack this city? What madness compelled you to do so?"

"We were commanded so," the man who sat next to Dale said as he placed a hand on Dale's chest.

"He would've never done that."

"Would he? I wonder, is it because both of you were from the same village? Is that why you think you are worthy of his sword?" the man asked.

"And you are?" Griffyn wondered.

"Edgar Rayle, of the Light," he said as he kept his gaze fixed on Griffyn.

"Of the Light?" Griffyn repeated as his brows narrowed. "Where's Kaven?"

"He's rather occupied with other matters for now."

"I think we're getting a bit sidetracked here," Wilson finally broke his silence. "Why did you summon this meeting, Edgar of the Light?"

Edgar sighed. "I summoned you here to quietly ask you to retreat. We've another battle to prepare for, and if you remain here, you will be exposed."

"And just who might you be preparing to fight?" Griffyn asked as he kept his gaze fixed on Edgar.

Edgar took a quick glance at Dale. "You know, I can see why he irritates you," he said as he turned his gaze back to Griffyn. "There are far more things at play here. A child like you will never understand the concept—"

"That's just the thing," Griffyn cut him off. "You all like to pretend that only you two lost someone who was important to you." He drove the Masamune in the ground a bit further and walked towards them. "When will you realize that the world far surpasses your agony!" he shouted.

The words drove a knife into Edgar's heart. "And what do you know of sacrifice?"

"I was there," Griffyn repeated. "On the day my best friend was killed, and our First Sword was put to death. I was there, Edgar..." he muttered as his voice broke down. "And it was your commander who laid his life so that I may escape."

Edgar stood up and came down of the carriage. "You say that, but we only have your word. And I can't help wonder why he would lay his life down to save a little arrogant punk like you," Edgar said.

"Test me, and find out." Griffyn replied, not breaking eye contact. Tension rose through the air.

"So, this enemy you're preparing to fight, I assume it's that demonic army we defeated at Lake Vita," Wilson intercepted.

Edgar's eyes shifted towards him. "Lake Vita?"

"Yes, and we quashed them thoroughly. So, you needn't worry about them at all."

Dale smirked at him. "Those you fought were the scouts. You see, they're far too organized to be called a horde. They operate as any professional army would. They send scouts, and then strategize."

"That's impossible," Wilson said.

"Is it?" Edgar challenged. "How do you justify their existence then?"

"If that's the case, then it's all the more reason we should join forces." Griffyn said, and both Edgar and Dale sighed.

"That is not an option."

"Gentlemen," Wilson said as he approached them slowly. "We have to admit that when it comes to demons, our inner conflicts can pause for a little while."

"No," Edgar said as he shifted his gaze back to Griffyn. "Heed my warning, and pull your armies back, lest we burn you all to the ground."

"Go ahead. Give the order," Griffyn said.

Edgar shook his head and entered the carriage again. "You have three hours," he said as he signaled with his hand, and the carriage made way back to Wynne.

"Why did you do that?" Wilson asked.

Griffyn pondered a moment, and then looked at Wilson. "He said 'of the light' that's why."

"I beg your pardon?"

"All soldiers of the Red Hand say 'of the light, by the light' that is their... identification method. This proves there's a dispute amongst them."

Wilson scratched his lower chin. "It's not uncommon for the death of a commander to separate his forces."

"But if that's true, they don't have the fire power we imagined. Half of that army is either imprisoned or rebelling."

Wilson stared at Griffyn for a moment. "It's striking how one moment you behave like a child, and the next you have analyzed a situation better than seasoned generals," Wilson added. "But still, we need to head back."

Griffyn sighed as he stepped towards the horse. "Let's head back then. I believe there are a lot more things we need to discuss."

Wilson smiled and got on the horse. Griffyn took his hand, and they both rode back towards their camp.

# CHAPTER 15

## *Blood for Blood*

Inside the tent, Wilson kept his gaze on Griffyn who had his hands placed on a table that had a map of their surroundings. A few other soldiers were with them.

"Well? What do you propose?" Wilson asked one of the soldiers. "I think it is best to stick to our original plan, starve them out."

"That would work," Griffyn said as he paused. "If you forgot about the demon army marching at our backs."

Wilson struck his hand on the table. "Out, all of you," he shouted, and all soldiers left the tent hastily. Griffyn began to move towards the exit.

"Not you," Wilson said as Griffyn halted. "Do you really believe their words to be true? A fucking demon army?"

"Considering that one already attacked the Citadel, yes, it's possible," Griffyn stated as he looked at Wilson. "It is also possible that the search party have—"

"Don't say it," Wilson cut him off. "Just don't," he said as he tilted his head towards Griffyn. "I ought to relieve all my advisors and keep you instead."

"I doubt you'd be able to handle my charming attitude all the time."

"You may be right. If the search party somehow got ambushed by demons, it would only make sense to send another. Only this time, I think we should send our best."

"Are you saying what I think you're saying?"

Wilson stood straight. "I think we have few choices left."

"About time—"

"Captain!" a soldier burst through the flap of the tent. "We're under attack!" the soldier cried at the top of his lungs.

Wilson and Griffyn took a good hard look at him. "By who?" Wilson uttered.

"The Red Hand's army! They have—"

"Show me," Wilson demanded as he hurried towards the exit.

Griffyn followed them, but Wilson placed a hand his

chest. "Not this time," Wilson said as he paused and smiled. "You stay here."

Griffyn glared at him. He knew there was something more behind Wilson's words and actions. Could Wilson be trusting him to take over if the worst comes to pass?

"Wilson..."

"I've led dozens of battles. You know strategy, I'll give you that, but I fought a war not long ago with these men. I know their every move. Have faith, will you?"

"Stay here and do what?"

"Think," Wilson said as he stepped outside.

\* \* \*

Wilson stepped outside, and immediately, the air around him became thicker. It almost smelled like ash. He stared as the archers atop the walls began shooting their fire arrows at them. Yet there was still some form of dysfunction amongst them. Not all archers fired at once.

"Bastards!" Wilson shouted as he held the back of his head. Soldiers were running about, shouting and trying to make sense of this sudden attack.

Wilson took a good look at his surroundings. "Fall in line!" he bellowed at them. Soldiers quickly rallied near him.

"Sir, what will we do?" one of the soldiers asked.

"Why are they firing at us like this?"

"They intend to make sacrifices of us all," Wilson explained as he pointed towards the opened doors. "See there? They intend to form a wall of fire and have us slow down whatever is marching to our south," Wilson said as he tried reading the strategy as best as he could.

The soldiers kept forming a line. Swords were pouring at the front, and at their middle, spearmen were at the ready with cavalries guarding the flanks.

"We won't make it. Not in time," Wilson said. Rush towards the gate. If we get too close, they will not fire, Wilson remembered. "I can't believe I am listening to him, again."

Wilson took a good look at his soldiers. "My soldiers, look at your iron shields, for beyond them are your enemies. They intend to drive fear into your hearts," he said as he put his hand on his chest. "That very same fear that I feel now. But do not fret, do not falter. We will be victorious!" Wilson cheered as the soldier's roars became louder.

"Storm the gate! Get behind their range!" Wilson shouted as the soldiers all glanced at each other. "Charge!" Wilson bellowed as hard as he could and rushed towards the open gates.

Soldiers quickly followed after their captain.

The faster they charged towards the gates, the sooner archers would load up the arrows and fire them, but then they halted for a moment. Wilson gazed at the horizon, as its colors changed. It became the color of fury, as he saw the archers ignite the tips of their arrows and prepare to release.

Shit, it was a trap, he thought to himself. They were only pretending to fire.

"Soldiers!" Wilson cried at the top of his lunges. "Shields!" he shouted unto them. Yet only those close to him listened. They halted, and lifted their shields to guard against the barrage of arrows that descended upon them.

Yet not all had shields. The cavalry was routed as some arrows hit the soldiers and others struck their horses. Fire began to spread. The battlefield was filled with cries and tears. Wilson pondered for a moment. The stench of rotting flesh engulfed him. His tactic worked for the moment only.

From the corner of his eye, he saw a spearman that was engulfed in flames. He was shouting. Wilson squinted, and as soon as the arrows seized, he lowered the iron shield of his and tossed his sword at the spearman.

The sword pierced his head.

"Charge! Do not falter!" Wilson cried as he ran again. His gaze tilted and fixated on the archers. Is this it? Is it by fire that I perish? Wilson's eyes widened. How beautiful it seems, he thought as he smiled from ear to ear. A tear ran down his cheek. Death seemed so simple in that instance.

He saw the archers reload. They readied the next wave

of arrows, and just as they lifted their bows into the air, Wilson halted. All of those who hadn't been already burned paused alongside with him.

It was as if time slowed down. Yet, on the walls, he noticed someone new had just appeared. The archers were awaiting his command. "Dale..." he whispered as he turned around and looked at his soldiers.

"What is your name?" he asked one of them.

"Rin, sir..." the soldier said.

"That's a beautiful name, soldier," he said as he paused. "And you?" he asked another.

"Stone, Captain... Deviline Stone..." the soldier answered, then sighed. "Fighting alongside you has been the honor of my life, sir." She said as her eyes dilated.

"The honor is mine," Wilson said as his voice broke down. He fell to his knees, coughing. The smoke from the fires that burned his soldiers was getting to him. "This is..." he muttered as he lifted his head and looked at Dale a final time.

Dale stared directly at him. He smirked and lowered his hand. A second barrage of fire arrows descended upon Wilson and his soldiers. Wilson, with all the strength that he could muster, lifted his shield. "May we meet again," he prayed as he hid his face behind the shield.

Every moment felt like an eternity. He could almost hear his heartbeats through his throat. He braced himself and gritted his teeth. He shouted in defeat, but as he did, he felt a gentle breeze pass by him. It was cold.

He removed his shield and found that the arrows never touched them. As if a giant wind hit them midair and blew them away. "What is going on?" he asked as he looked left.

Wilson then glanced to his right, "Rin, Deviline... get up!" he demanded. But he didn't get a response. They were both laying face down. He threw his shield and crawled towards them. "Soldiers!" he shouted yet again. He placed his hand on their necks, trying to feel a pulse.

He gritted his teeth as his brows narrowed. He punched the ground repeatedly "Why! Why!" he shouted. But then he heard a voice; a horse, jogging as fast as it could. It got faster and faster. He looked back, and saw it was Griffyn atop the horse, riding towards the gate.

"Wait!" Wilson shouted but wasn't heard.

He kept his gaze fixated as Griffyn passed him. He held the Masamune in his right hand. Wilson quickly averted his eyes towards Dale. They were moving frantically. Dale was barking orders at the archers to try again, but something had changed.

Only half the archers loaded again and fired at Griffyn. "Watch out!" Wilson shouted at him, but then Griffyn swung the Masamune in a flawless motion. Wind seemed to fire from his sword and blew the arrows away.

"Is this... real?" Wilson uttered. Griffyn reached the gate, but he seemed to stop. "Why is this idiot getting off his horse?" He almost didn't believe his eyes.

He then saw Griffyn lift the Masamune in the air, pointing it at Dale. He heard him shout "Blood for blood!"

# CHAPTER 16

## *Boy*

No one anticipated it. Griffyn waited outside the walls of Wynne, the archers had stopped. They witnessed something they only read about in books. Not all who served under the Red Hand saw his Titan Power, so this came as a shock to both those who did see his powers and those who didn't.

Dale's brows rose high as his jaw dropped.

"Come down!" Griffyn shouted as he looked at him. His pupils dilated and veins formed on his forehead. "Step down, or I will bring this city to its knees, and you with it."

Dale snapped out of his shock. He saw a boy that had outlived his commander using the same power. "You dare threaten me with my commander's sword?"

"Come down and take it," Griffyn shot at him with a

blank face. In that instant, his pupils sparked. An orange hue wrapped his iris's and then flashed blue before returning back to normal.

Dale pondered for a moment, then disappeared from the wall. Moments after, he came outside surrounded by a dozen guards who formed a circle between Dale and Griffyn.

The guards were prepared for battle, and were dressed in full plate armor. Griffyn scanned them quickly, they had no visible weak points. If Dale wasn't skilled enough, surely his guards would be.

But then again, he has never fought, nor seen, Dale in action. "I don't know what stupid thoughts dwell within your brain, but if you think you can end this quickly, I assure you, you can't." Dale said.

"Still your tongue," Griffyn spat as he shifted his gaze towards Dale. "You've spilled more blood than I have, but there is no reality where you walk away after what you did."

Dale averted his eyes towards Wilson. "Does he know what you are? Does he know about your compulsion?"

Griffyn shook his head. "Your attempts at diverting what becomes of you will be in vain."

"You dare cast judgment as if you are my lord. Know this, boy, the only man I knelt to is the same man whose sword you wield."

Griffyn smirked at Dale. "If he had lived to see what

you've done, he would've killed you where you stand."

Dale's head shook gently as veins popped on his forehead. He unsheathed his sword. "Before this day is passed, I will cut out your tongue and feed it to your friend."

"Step forth Dale, of the Light." Griffyn said.

Dale rushed Griffyn and swung to the side. Griffyn parried, a clash of swords rang out through the air. Griffyn didn't budge, he was smaller and lighter.

Dale swung repeatedly, but Griffyn matched his form.

Until you see the world in forms, Griffyn remembered what Rory had told Vendel when she was teaching her swordplay. He could see it clearly.

Griffyn dashed to the right and swung at Dale's armor, but Dale managed to dodge and hold his arm. He applied as much pressure as he could, but Griffyn wouldn't let go of the Masamune.

A blade isn't the only weapon on the sword, he remembered what Wilson had said to him. He struck his head against Dale's, pushing him away.

"Trickery, coward... you would have me believe the Red Hand himself gave his sword to someone like you?" Dale shouted as he shook his head. He put all of his strength into his next swing.

Griffyn had only one choice. He reversed Dale's swing and, as the Masamune clashed with Dale's sword, the latter broke.

Dale fell on his face.

# TITANLORD

"Why did you do this? What would the Red Hand think?" Griffyn said as he stepped closer to Dale. "What would Natasha think? What would Tatiana think of you right this moment!" Griffyn's voice rose towards the end.

"She's dead!" Dale cried at the top of his lungs as he pushed his face against the dirt. Griffyn's mouth laid wide open. "They raped her, and then they decapitated her, and hung her head on top of the walls, Griffyn..." Dale added as his voice broke.

"What?" Griffyn uttered.

"That is why we marched here in the first place, to burn Wynne to the ground for what they did... That is what Ben would've done..."

"No..."

"He would! Because Ben understood that justice went beyond the benefits of one person or another. It was absolute... that is what he taught us, and that is why I wanted to avenge her..."

Griffyn shook his head. "Vengeance is not justice. I'm sorry for your loss," Griffyn held his chest. He felt his heart racing. Tatiana had saved him and Rory before. He owed her his life. Back when he was in Fort Eldren he had asked Tatiana to join, but she wouldn't put him at risk.

"You've been hurting, carrying all this burden alone, haven't you?" Griffyn asked as he eyed Dale.

Dale nodded. "I couldn't save my own sister... If she had only listened to me and let me accompany her, then none of this would've happened... Do you understand?"

Griffyn looked at the ground and sighed. He pointed back at Wilson and the remnants of the army. "What of them?" he whispered. "Dale, what of the people you slaughtered without cause, without anything?"

Dale turned his face and gritted his teeth.

"How did you come to the decision that their lives were worth forfeiting?" Griffyn said, his tone a bit sharper. "By what right do you commit genocide only to condemn it?" Griffyn added. "By what right!" he shouted as he pointed the Masamune at Dale.

"Guards!" Dale shouted. All soldiers but one unsheathed their sword and came rushing at Griffyn.

Griffyn waved the Masamune and a giant wind swept nearly all the soldiers off their feet. Dale covered his face with his hands.

"I told you. You took the blood of the innocent. There is no reality in which you walk away alive," Griffyn threatened and then shifted his gaze towards the soldiers. "Still your blades. Your hands are clean, for now," he said.

"Looking away when fighting a duel to the death? Not a good idea, boy," he heard Dale say as he was suddenly standing next to him. A dagger to his throat.

Don't move. Griffyn heard clearly at the back of his head. "Trickery and cowardice, are those the terms you used?"

"That sword does not belong to you," Dale said as he

pried the Masamune from Griffyn's hand. "War spares not the brave, but the cowardly," Dale said.

"What a stupid soldier you are," Griffyn said.

"Don't worry, I will avenge the Red Hand, and Tatiana, and all those who fell. I will end it all, that I swear to you."

"An oath from a killer weighs little on my conscious. Mind you, it's not your fault but mine for believing you to have a shred of honor."

Dale smiled. "I don't entirely hate you, you know, but I've come too far to stop now. Like you said, too many innocents have died for me to simply fall to my knees and ask for forgiveness."

"Dale, it's not too late. You can end all of this, just put down your weapon, and face your fate."

"From who? You?"

"Whoever it may be."

Dale smiled. "I think not," he said as he applied a bit of pressure to the dagger. "So long, little... soldier, what are you do-"

Dale placed a hand on his own neck. A dagger had pierced it. The soldier who stayed back and didn't attack Griffyn had moved quietly, waiting for the right moment. "You... fucking... traitor..." he gurgled as he fell to the ground. He tried to stop the blood pouring from his neck with his hands.

"'He who lays hands on this sword without cause,

seize him. He who forsakes the light, kill him'" the soldier said. "Do you recall what I just said? And who indeed said it, Dale Hunter, Captain of the Light?" the soldier asked as he removed his helmet.

"Kaven..." Griffyn whispered.

"The only traitors here are those who aided you," he said as he took a deep breath and stared at the guards who were just getting up.

"By my order, General Kaven Holt, I command you all to surrender," Kaven demanded, and the soldiers obeyed. He stepped towards the Masamune and picked it up. He then offered it to Griffyn. "Ben would never give his sword willingly, and if he did, then he would have his own reason."

Griffyn's gaze shifted towards Wilson.

"I swear to you that those who were involved will answer to justice," Kaven said as he lowered his head.

"What are you... doing?" Griffyn gawked at him.

The guards stood their ground. Though dressed in armor, their gasps could be heard clearly. "On behalf of those who still walk within the light, please accept my apologies."

# CHAPTER 17

## *By The Light*

Flourishing as it once was, silence hovered atop of Wynne; a village on the way to becoming a city. The gates led a straight path towards the keep, with the market district on the right and houses on the left.

Griffyn stood in the center of what appeared to be the courtyard. Wilson stood beside him, overlooking all the archers who partook in the massacre that just occurred. Kaven stood in front of Griffyn.

"How many survived?" Griffyn asked Wilson.

"Not many. All those who had shields fared better, but fire is not prone to contact alone. Some of them survived, but the arrows touched the ground near them and the fire caught on the grass and their clothes. We were..." Wilson explained as he took a pause and lowered his face. "...utterly decimated."

Griffyn placed a hand on his shoulder. "Don't be so hard on yourself. The lives they gave will be a constant reminder for you not to forget them, honor them."

Wilson's brows narrowed, but the thin line in his lips formed into a smile. "Thank you, Griffyn... I don't know what to make of anything anymore. I think I need to rest."

"You'll have all the time you need, but first...we deal with this," Griffyn said as he nodded at Kaven.

Kaven nodded back and turned to face the archers. He looked at his surroundings. Soldiers, guards, and any who lived in Wynne came to see the trial.

"You all stand accused of treason. By the laws put forward by the First, and then acknowledged by the Second—"

"Then you would stand beside us!" one of the archers shouted.

"You betrayed the Red Hand just as much as Dale had. If anyone deserves to die, it's you!" another added.

Kaven's brows narrowed. "You dishonor yourselves," he said as he took a step closer to them. "Why do we exist?" he asked. "Are we some common bandits who sack a city, and then turn to fire to attack someone needlessly?"

"You bowed to that boy just now, how exactly are you any different?" one of the archers argued.

# TITANLORD

Kaven tried to speak but felt Griffyn's gentle hand on his shoulder and paused.

"Allow me to intervene," Griffyn said.

"By what right?" the archer shot back at him.

Griffyn turned his gaze upon him, and in that he saw just how hollow his eyes were. Not a visible trace of fear or doubt lurked within them.

He drew the Masamune and stuck it into the ground, holding its hilt with a steady hand. "By this right in particular," he said to them as silence gloomed. It was a knife to the heart for most of them.

"None of you were there, when the Gods descended and laid waste to the Capital. None of you saw how bravely Ben fought, and how he died for one purpose: for us to survive," he said as his brows neared. "Yet I ask you, as you asked me before, by what right did you forsake honor and resort to trickery?" he asked them, and their faces went pale.

"By what right did you all decide to kill us when you knew we weren't the enemy?" he continued. "Ben, your commander, Rory, the First Sword of Palleria, and Vendel all gave their lives away so that humanity may live on and fight for the very right to exist, yet you dare stand atop a pile of graves and make noises about how you were insulted, and how you were done wrong.

"What of the hearts that perished because of you? What are the ghosts in your minds telling you about them?

Do they tell you you're innocent? Or do they try to convince you that this is but a dream?"

Wilson squinted his eyes and took a hard look at Griffyn. Is this truly the boy I found running away from the Capital? He thought to himself.

A thin smile formed on Kaven's face as he took a few steps forward. "Our law is clear. Justice above all. It is with that rule that I turn now to you two," he paused as he faced Wilson and Griffyn. "I leave it in your hands," he said as his heartbeat raced higher.

Wilson leaned towards Griffyn. "This was your victory. You call it," he said to him as he crossed his arms.

Griffyn nodded as he took another step closer to the archers. He paused for a moment and took a deep breath. He felt the air shift in his surroundings. His words were harsh, but he knew that he spoke the truth. The cold hard truth. "I didn't mean to wound," he said as he placed his hand on the back of his head. "I am trying to think of what the Red Hand would do, were he in my position..." he added.

Upon mentioning this, Griffyn noticed the archers grew timid. Tension rose in the courtyard. "But I must take actions with my own hands. Blood for blood," he stated as he shifted his gaze and took a look at Kaven.

Veins beaded on Kaven's forehead. He paused for a moment and swallowed. "Then it is settled," he said as he looked at the archers. "Your lives are forfeit."

The air seemed thick around Griffyn, the tension could

cut it with a knife. He gazed upon the faces of those he condemned. It was only justice, he said to himself.

The gates of Wynne opened then. All who gathered turned towards the iron gate. Kaven, Griffyn, and Wilson made haste. "By whose command did you open the gate?" Kaven shouted.

"They were asking for a Wilson, General," one of the soldiers shouted.

Griffyn and Wilson exchanged glances. Wilson rushed outside. "Let them in!" he shouted.

Kaven clicked his tongue. "You heard him."

The soldier rushed inside as he panted heavily. His armor was pierced and his rags torn. "Captain," he exhaled as he collapsed.

Wilson caught him, "Easy there, soldier," Wilson said, looking him in the eye. "Medic!" he shouted as he glanced at Kaven. "What did this to you?"

"They're... coming..." he stuttered as he exhaled and his body seemed to be lighter, turning cold in Wilson's arms.

Kaven turned towards Griffyn whose eyes flared a light blue. "Demons..." he heard Griffyn whisper out of tone, his pupils returning to normal.

"Get him inside," Wilson commanded to one of the gatekeepers and then turned. "We need to prepare for a siege."

The townsfolks of Wynne seemed to scatter against the

winds as they hurled into a panic. They hid in their homes, with children being left and separated from their parents. All save for the soldiers, who remained calm and steady.

Wilson walked towards Griffyn and touched his shoulder. "I know what you're thinking, and you aren't necessarily wrong, but now is not the time for doubt."

"I should've gone with them..." Griffyn mumbled, his eyes wide. "Maybe then we could've..."

"Griffyn," Wilson said as he shook him. "Now we fight. Should we emerge victorious after this, then we will have the time to mourn for as long as we want."

Griffyn shook his head. The two of them looked to Kaven.

Kaven took a deep breath. "Which of you has more experience?" He asked them with straight face.

"To lead?" Wilson asked, then Kaven glanced at Griffyn, who nodded in agreement. Kaven would be their best choice. "A general of the Red Hand is perhaps our best option." Wilson added.

"We will live through this," Kaven said as he turned away from Wilson and Griffyn. The soldiers were gathered around him, awaiting his command. "There's no time to do a perimeter. Man the walls and gather everyone in the courtyard," he commanded as he looked at Griffyn. "What do you think we should do?"

Griffyn raised a brow. "I would imagine there's a secret tunnel of some sort. Something that we can use to our advantage."

"You're probably right, but we just recently took this town... or city. We didn't have the proper time to inspect everything."

"What about their people? Or the previous guards?" Wilson asked.

Kaven took a deep breath. "All the guards were executed."

Wilson raised a brow. He was about to speak when Griffyn placed a hand on his chest. "Later," he said before sighing. "I assume military secrets of the location remain... secret to the townsfolks then."

Kaven nodded. "If you would like to, I'll spare a few soldiers so you can look for that advantage."

"No," Wilson jumped in. "You saw what he can do," he said as he took a few steps forward. "Don't make the same mistake that I did."

Griffyn kept quiet. He didn't mind doing either. Of course, he leaned towards fighting alongside everyone else, but if there was one thing he remembered from Rory, it was that strength alone cannot bring victory.

"How about you look for the passage?" Kaven said as he turned and faced Wilson. He stared at him for a while. "It's the best chance we got," Kaven added as his attention shifted.

"General," a soldier shouted as he rushed towards them.

"Report," Kaven replied.

The soldier paused for a moment, he swallowed. "We're running out of time, General..." he said as the air thickened around them.

"Grab a dozen more soldiers, and you are to accompany this man here," Kaven said as he pointed towards Wilson.

"That won't be necessary," Wilson said. "My men will do," he added before he turned around. "We've bled, won, and lost together. We'll find this secret passage," he committed, nodding his head.

"How will you know when to strike?" Griffyn asked Wilson.

"He can read the battle as it goes," Kaven explained as he approached Wilson and extended his hand. "We may have been enemies at the beginning, but this war that has come, it comes for us all."

Wilson looked at him from the corner of his eye. "Whatever may come, we will withstand and outlive it," Wilson said as he turned to face Kaven. "But even now, though we fight together, we are still enemies," he added as he locked his gaze with Kaven's. "Don't forget that... 'General'" he mocked and shook his hand.

"I won't," Kaven said with a smile.

The ground beneath their feet shook. "Go!" Kaven shouted at his men as he turned and ran towards the wall. "You, come with me," he said as he pointed towards

# TITANLORD

Griffyn.

Griffyn nodded and the two of them reached the top of the wall shortly. Their gazes fell upon the horizon. There was a deafening silence that gloomed. Ash tainted their lips, making their mouths dry and gritty.

"Why is it so quiet suddenly?" Griffyn wondered as his heart began to pound in his chest. He looked at Kaven and saw him scanning his surroundings.

Soldiers were buzzing in and out of position. There was panic and chaos happening around them. For some odd reason, the unified and strong army of the Red Hand seemed clueless.

"What's going on?"

Kaven swallowed the lump in his throat as he pointed towards the horizon. "What do you see?" he asked.

"Nothing," Griffyn replied with a shrug.

"Look closer."

Griffyn squinted his eyes to make out the details of a figure at least ten miles away. He seemed fixed on the ground; it was hardly visible, save for two dots where its eyes should have been.

"What...is that!" Griffyn gawked as the ground shook again. "It's moving towards us," Griffyn's brows rose.

"Back when you used the Commander's powers," Kaven said as his gaze remained fixed on the figure that was approaching. "Can you use them again?"

"I can," Griffyn replied as he took a deep breath. "But I can't control it."

"Well," Kaven said as he crossed his arms. "You're going to have to try, otherwise—"

Kaven paused as the being halted next to a boulder. It seemed to crouch for a moment, and then picked up the giant rock as an adult would lift a child.

"What's it doing?" Griffyn asked.

"Is this real?" Kaven let loose a breath with his words. He looked closer as the being hurled the boulder towards them. There was a great distance between them, but the boulder shot towards them as sharp as an arrow.

"Brace yourselves! Get down! Get down!" Kaven shouted at the top of his lungs. He pushed Griffyn's head down. There was panic, but then silence.

Griffyn's heartbeats pounded in his ears. If there was one thing that was more terrifying than knowing that something was coming, it was not knowing when exactly it would come.

A thudding noise tore at the wall. The stone danced against the contact, the concrete shifting, as rubble began to pile up and cover the entire wall and gate.

"We're dead... we can't do this!" one of the soldiers cried.

"Not without the commander... this is insanity!" another chimed in.

"Do not falter!" Kaven shouted at the soldiers as he

covered his head with both hands.

"We won't last like this!" Griffyn shouted as he looked at Kaven "We have to take the fight to them," he said as he averted his gaze.

"We won't survive a minute outside," Kaven explained. "Many will die..."

"And many more will if we stay our hands and wait for them near the gate," he said before he paused. "This whole place will fall. They're not here to fight fairly."

"How can we even get close? We will be smashed to pieces..."

Griffyn stood and closed his eyes. He lifted his sword. "Please work, please..." he said under his breath. He opened his eyes just in time; that thing was about to hurl another boulder.

Griffyn lifted the Masamune with all his might and let out a cry at the top of his lungs as he swung it. Yet nothing happened. His pupils dilated as he saw the boulder getting closer.

"Get down!" Kaven cried as he tackled Griffyn to the ground. The boulder hit the wall towards their right. It was closer to them this time. "Are you trying to get yourself killed?" Kaven shouted.

"Why should I?" Griffyn asked before he covered his mouth again. The dust and rubble reached them once more. "What did Ben use to do? Do you have any idea?"

"How am I supposed to know? Didn't you just use it

on the arrows?" Kaven shouted. "This is pointless...We are not trained to battle monsters," doubt began to seep into Kaven's heart.

Griffyn took a good look at him. "Battling monsters isn't as important as standing up to them," Griffyn said as his voice broke down. He stood yet again.

"Don't be an idiot..." Kaven spat.

"You said it yourself, these are monsters," Griffyn said as he shifted his gaze towards the horizon. "If we intend to take on the extraordinary, we ourselves cannot be ordinary," he claimed as he lifted the Masamune again.

He waited for the being to lift another boulder and swung his sword just when it tossed the boulder. The wind came out this time, and the gust met the large rock in mid-air.

The collision sent a wave that echoed across the entire region. Soldiers cowered, covering their pained ears from the sound. Rocks rained down, clambering to the earth below in a shattering storm. Large gouges were scratched into the surface from the force of the blow.

Griffyn stood still, then shifted his gaze towards the skies. "The sky... it's split..." he said under his breath and then turned towards the soldiers.

Two hearts, Griffyn heard clear in his head. His brows narrowed, then he looked back at Kaven. "It is not about survival, or battle... when you face atrocities like these, the most important thing is for you to stand up to them," he said as Kaven's pupils dilated.

Griffyn shifted his gaze towards the soldiers yet again. "So long as I live," he paused to lift his sword. "So long as I hold this sword that was given to me by your commander," he continued as he took a few steps forward. "Hope will never be lost."

The soldiers cheered. To them this was an important tribute, a reminder that their commander did not abandon them, and that through Griffyn's actions, he lives.

Griffyn studied the soldiers who had celebrated. As he scanned the faces of the soldiers that he was fighting hand in hand with, he noticed a few familiar faces.

It's the archers, he thought to himself. The archers he condemned to death, to his dismay, did not use the chaos to escape, but chose to stay and fight.

He couldn't help but smile. As the going got tougher, it was important to see that the people around him didn't lose faith. His strike proved essential not only to those soldiers, but rather to himself as well. It showed that he hadn't given up when he had all the reason in the world to do so.

He shot the archers a cold stare, and they froze where they stood. Some of them lowered their gazes to the ground.

"Griffyn," Kaven said as he stepped closer towards the edge of the wall. "It stopped."

"What do you mean?"

"It stopped throwing those damn boulders, that's what I mean," he said as he balled his hand into a fist. "It worked. I think they're worried that you'll just push whatever they throw back at them."

Griffyn scratched his lower chin and walked closer. "Then they agree with us; we should settle this outside."

"I'm not entirely sure our chances are far better out there."

"There's only one way to find out," Griffyn shrugged as he turned around and glanced back at the soldiers. He nodded at those who looked at him, and then shifted his gaze back towards Kaven. "Prepare to charge."

# CHAPTER 18

## *Mutiny*

Opsis was under fire. Soldiers rushed towards the walls while others were running across the city, evacuating everyone they could. Dust filled the place as rubble rose towards knee level. "Where the hell is Kog?" wondered a man as he grabbed one of the soldiers running about.

"Up there," the soldier pointed at the wall.

The man rushed through the stairs; his chest heaved from exertion. He took a breath. "Kog!" he shouted.

Kog had his gaze fixed on the horizon. A sea of darkness had been approaching the city. It was slow, but with every step the horde took, doubt began to seek into the back of his mind. Can mortals even win such a fight? He thought to himself.

"Look at these fuckers," Kog mumbled. "Tell me, what the fuck do you see? Or do your clothes cover your dick too much for you to see what I see?"

"I've seen you win every battle you've ever fought. You aren't about to lose heart just yet, are you?"

Kog shook his head. "You're still too stupid to realize that we lost this war the second the fuckers decided to march down on us."

"This is Ospis!" the man fought. "It has yet to fall!"

Kog covered his head with both hands. "Why the fuck are you here? If you aren't man enough to pick up a sword, then go hide with the women and children."

The man's eyes seemed to grow heavy. "You will take us out of this. We all believe in you."

"A city of thieves believes in me, how ironic," Kog said as he turned his head to the right "On my command!" he yelled, and all archers pulled their arrows as far back as they could.

"Look at them, memorize their faces, for if you fall today, they will not stop with your measly lives, but will turn to those who you hold dear. Ospis has been a mother to us all... fight for her!"

The soldiers roared as the horde approached.

"Now!" Kog gave the command, and a burst of arrows shot towards the horde. A sound of reckoning was edged into the back of everyone's mind. The sound of steel clashing against something far more unnatural than anything they have ever witnessed before.

The Dwellers shrieked at the impact as they broke formation. Each and every one of them rushed towards the wall in a demonic sprint.

Kog took a few steps back. His mouth wide open. "They don't care whether they live or die..." Kog gasped for a moment.

"What's going on!" the man asked.

Kog turned, and saw the man had laid down on the ground covering his face. Kog shook his head. "Militia, on me!" he shouted as he ran down and faced the gate.

"If any of you has any gods you pray to, cling to them. This is an hour unlike any you have ever seen. If they won't help you keep the gate closed, then what good are the cunts?"

Every soldier there pressed their bodies and everything else they had against the gate; they had to keep it secured. "If they breach the gate, the city will be lost!" Kog bellowed.

"Sir! They are not going towards the gate!" one of the archers shouted. Kog tilted his head just enough to make out his details from the corner of his eyes. A Dweller then jumped upwards and landed on the archer, sinking its teeth into his chest.

"What in the fuck is that..." Kog pondered as he ran towards the stairs again. With every step he took, more and more Dwellers jumped inwards, landing on the battlements. "How!" he shouted as he took out his axe and swung it, cutting through a Dweller. He reached the edge of the wall and leaned forward.

He gawked, his jaw nearly touching the floor. Those hideous dark creatures were stepping on one another, creating a live ladder. Thousands of demonic bodies scrambled up the wall, each getting higher as the numbers in the ladder grew. He took a few steps back and paused when he hit something. He turned around and heard the sounds of a man crying.

"I don't want to die, not yet..." the man spout.

"Get up, and get back inside where it's safe—"

Kog gasped for air as one of the Dwellers jumped and drove its long nails into his side. "You sack of shit..." he mumbled under his breath as he grabbed the Dweller with both hands and squeezed as hard as he could. Kog pushed him off and held it in midair, "You're on the wrong side of the wall," he spat and threw the Dweller over the side. His eyes caught a glimpse of the sea of darkness that had descended upon them.

"Fuck me, this is one shitty way to die..." he said and took a few steps back. He turned and sprinted down to stand near his men. "Everyone gather around me!" he yelled, and the others obeyed.

"Are we letting them just... get inside?" a soldier questioned.

# TITANLORD

Kog shot the man a stare. "If they aren't using the gate, then only so much of them can actually make it over. If that happens, then our best bet is for all of us to fight majority of them right here."

"Are we going to die?" the man tried to catch his breath as panic bubbled over.

Kog nodded. "It could've been a day before, or a year after. It makes no sense to dwell on it now. Stand up."

The man swallowed and tightened his grip on the sword, but the rattling noise gave his heart away.

Kog looked at him. "What's your name, son?"

"Petersen, sir..." he muttered.

Kog placed a hand on his shoulder. "You've been brave, far braver than many others, I'd say, even those who sit at the council."

"It's been an honor, sir."

Kog tilted his head slowly towards the wall. The Dwellers seemed to crawl over them with ease. Then a horn blew. "What the fuck is it now?" Kog swore and took a deep breath.

"Sir, that horn..."

Kog gritted his teeth. "So, he sacked the city once, and now returns to do what?" he wondered as a raging sound of steel resonated through the surroundings. The sound of men roaring came from behind the wall themselves.

"It's him, isn't it? The devil is back!" The man held his

head as his eyes bewildered. "No one can save us now...not even those things out there!"

"Calm yourself," Kog shouted as he scanned his surroundings. That horn, whomever it came from, casted not only doubt within everyone's mind but also fear. A wreathing fire that ate at their pride. "Hold your position!" he shouted yet again, but his eyes laid on his hands.

They were shaking. He gasped. "The city that has never fallen, but it did, only to that man... Fuck!"

The sound of steel clashing against flesh rose, as battle cries from the outside remained constant, and the sound of those Dwellers shrieking came to a grand halt.

"Is it over?" one of the soldiers asked.

Kog shook his head. "No, now it ends," he sighed, taking a deep breath. Silence radiated through the city. Kog didn't know what he was more concerned about, the demons or their unknown savior.

The horn blew again. The sound rang out and sent shivers down his spine. "But, if the devil saved us from demons, does that mean he isn't the devil anymore?"

Kog kept his gaze fixed on the gates. The siege of Ospis on his mind, that was a day he would never forget.

Everyone around Kog cheered. They threw their hands in the air while others kneeled and prayed to their gods. But not Kog.

"Let your commander come forth," a voice came from the other side of the wall.

Kog's face twitched as he looked at the man beside him. "Devils, demons, whether they be saviors or destroyers... they remain cunts," he spat on the ground before he scaled up the wall again.

He leaned over the edge and saw a man in white armor. He held his helmet in his arm. "My people here believe you to be some kind of savior," Kog called down to him.

"And you don't?"

"I've seen what saviors can do, when given the chance."

"And what will you do then, when faced with such?"

"You're a lot shorter than you used to be."

The man smiled. "The Red Hand is dead. I assume command in his place and return to you so that you may honor your oath to him."

Kog leaned back a bit, a chuckle escaping him. "You've come a long way to seek honor in a city of thieves, but I don't have to tell you that now, do I? What's your name?"

"Edgar Rayle."

"Edgar Rayle? What kind of a name is that? I'll tell you, an unremarkable and unmemorable one that's for sure. Where's the brown-haired woman? Is she dead?"

Edgar smirked and glanced at the ground before lifting his eyes to meet Kog's. "I haven't the time for games, sir," he said before raising two fingers at Kog. "Salvation or annihilation."

Kog narrowed his brows. "I beg your pardon?"

"Choose."

Kog shook his head. "We haven't the men to repel you, but you knew that as well." He took a step back. "I'm not sure what your goals are, but I alone cannot make that decision."

"Then take me to someone who can," Edgar demanded.

Kog nodded. "Your men will stay outside the gates. I will escort you personally and guarantee your safety. Will that suffice?" he asked.

Edgar took a second. "Three of my knights will accompany me. As you stated earlier, this remains Ospis. I've no doubt that you're a man of your words, but I'm afraid the same can't be said for everyone inside."

"Cheeky," Kog whispered under his breath. "Open the gate," he gave the command and winked at the gatekeeper. He stepped down to meet Edgar. The gate was being barged open.

Then, stepped forth Edgar Rayle. The closer he got, the better Kog could make out his details. Sparkling gray eyes, set a-symmetrically within their sockets. He had a birthmark on his left cheek.

"You aren't really dressed for the war you threaten," Kog said as he waved him inside, looking at his white cape that covered his body.

"I disagree. In battle, fortunes are not decided by who's the strongest, rather it's the most agile and adaptive who prevail."

"Learned that from your Commander, eh?"

Edgar stopped. His face turned and his eyes pierced the back of Kog's skull. "Don't."

Kog smirked. "For what it's worth, he was the best man I ever fought," he said as he kept walking. "Come on."

Edgar's brows rose, but he followed.

"Mind the mess, will you? It's not every day that someone besieges a city of thieves."

"I don't mind it actually," Edgar said, turning his head to take in his surroundings. The place was dusty; rubble seemed to cover at least one third of the city. Inside the gates, the square opened up to the stable that sat on the right and the marketplace opposite of that.

Beyond that were living quarters. "I don't see a barracks."

"We have none. All those who fight for Ospis are the ones living in it. We can't afford the luxury of picking who lives here, and we're fortunate enough that those who do, deem it worthy enough to enlist in the militia."

"I see," Edgar said. Their pace remained constant. They were going straight ahead as a tall building came into view. "Who are we seeing exactly?" he asked.

"Ospis is led by a council, comprised of those who outlasted everyone else."

"So, it's not run by merit, rather by an age factor?"

"Don't forget, to survive for so long in a city filled with criminals, thieves and cutthroats is an achievement in itself."

"You don't seem amused."

"I learned long ago that the only difference between a nobleman and a cutthroat is simply the way they speak."

Edgar smiled.

"We're here," Kog said as the two of them reached the steps of the main building overseeing the square. Kog opened the door and stepped inside.

"As you can...smell, the place smells like shit," he said as he cast his gaze upon a long rug that led to a double door. "The councilmen should be inside, debating whether I can properly fend off that horde we saw," Kog said as he opened the doors.

"Well, even if you had won that battle, I'm not sure—" Edgar was cut short when they laid eyes on the room.

Silence filled the air. Kog and Edgar looked at the giant table in the middle. Five men sat at the chairs around the table, but their heads were sticking out at odd angles. Red stained the grey walls of the room, puddles forming beneath the men's feet. Their eyes quickly fell to the thing that levitated in midair.

A soft glow echoed off its form. Its golden helmet covered only half of its face and white sparkling armor adorned the rest of its body. Over its shoulders, two wings sat neatly at its back.

The men with Edgar drew their swords, but both Kog and him stood as silent as the graves.

"They were brave men," the creature said.

"What... are you?" Kog mumbled.

"You foolishly accept that demon's dwell within these lands, but forsake entirely the concept of something more?" it asked.

"It's you, Nepherin, isn't it?" Edgar asked.

"Our King is rather occupied."

"What do you want?" Kog said.

The creature gazed into Edgar's eyes. "You assume the mantle of someone you shouldn't. Why is that exactly?"

Edgar tried to speak but spewed something unintelligible instead.

"Mortals are so amusing. I can understand why my brother deems it worthwhile to eradicate mankind once and for all. This planet has sinned for far too long."

"Again... what do you want?" Kog asked. His hands trembled and his stomach clenched as he watched the being.

The creature smiled. "The war will come to an end momentarily. But just as soon as the Titanlord loses his head, comes an instance in which we beg the question: what now? What becomes of you foul and sinful humans that dared oppose the Gods?"

"What will you ask of us?" Edgar finally broke his silence.

"Kneel."

"Come again?" Kog asked.

The creature's smile turned. A thin line shaped the left of its face as its eyes grew bigger. "You have been blessed with an opportunity to serve the Gods you so fought."

"I don't recall fighting anybody, let alone a God, if that's what you are," Kog said, but the moment those words parted his lips, his brows rose.

The creature tilted its head to the right a bit. "In days past, I would've ended you where you stood. But alas, a reckoning is upon us, and your life may yet prove useful-"

The creature shrieked in pain as it flung across the room. Its glowing changed, from emitting light around itself to a radiating blue one that filled the surrounding room.

Kog and Edgar covered their eyes. "What's happening?" Kog asked.

The creature's cries remained constant, but then the blue light faded, and it fell on its feet, shaking. It lifted its right hand and kept its gaze on its palm. "It's... broken..." it uttered before tilting its head towards Edgar and Kog.

# CHAPTER 19

*Dream*

Red and brown were the colors of the sky. The soldiers of the Red Hand began descending as they hurried out in formation. In front of them, Griffyn and Kaven stood still, awaiting whatever came their way.

"I hope you're right about this," Kaven said as he leaned closer towards Griffyn.

"It's pointless to say these things now," Griffyn stated as he kept his gaze fixed towards that monster.

The ground shook more frequently, and the closer it got, the louder the cries of those foul beings became. "Do you know what they are?"

"Dwellers, deformed zealots that worship the Titans."

"I see you had the crash course from Natasha," Kaven

smiled a bit. "But I'm guessing she didn't, did she?"

Griffyn shook his head.

"Well, if we survive this, then maybe I'll tell you the story," Kaven cracked his knuckles.

"Fine," Griffyn said as his eyes began to dilate. The ground kept shaking at a steady pace. Griffyn felt something that he hadn't felt in a long time. He looked down at his hands and tried to keep them still, but they wouldn't obey.

"I'm shaking..." he huffed under his breath.

"Good," Kaven said as he looked at him from the corner of his eye. "It means you're not stupid."

The dust clouds began to clear, and as the fog went away, the Dweller army appeared all around the giant that fast approached.

"Adducere..." The giant spoke as it halted and lifted its hands in the air. "Interfectorem de diis," it added, though its sound was so high pitched that it came off as just remarks.

"Did it...speak just now?" Kaven asked.

"I didn't understa-" Griffyn paused as he felt a tingle spread through his mind. Bring the killer of the Gods.

"Bring the killer of the Gods..." Griffyn repeated out loud.

"What?" Kaven asked as he drew his sword. "Is that what it said?"

"Yes."

"How did you... never mind, it doesn't matter right now. At least we know whose side they're on," Kaven said as he turned towards the soldiers. "Men of the Light," he ordered as he lifted his sword. "The time has come for you to prove your mettle right here, right now!"

Griffyn turned his head towards him.

"So many were taken from us, but that ends today. Let us begin first by killing these sons of whores who side with the killers of our commander," Kaven added as the soldiers stood still, their frozen feet shifted at his words.

A fire rekindled in their eyes. "Let no man fall today without knowing what we fight for," he paused as he took a deep breath. "For Benjen!" he cried at the top of his lungs and charged straight ahead.

Griffyn rushed alongside Kaven as the two led the vanguard. They were joined by a thunderous roar beside them. The fire raged inside each and every soldier. It was as if they didn't accept their commander's death and intended to fight for it.

"Leave the giant to me. The rest, do your best to clear a path!" Griffyn shouted to those nearby.

"Don't get killed, kid," Kaven said as the first crash of swords came to play. Kaven dodged a swing to the right and swung his sword upward. He appeared as though he was dancing. Every movement was fluid.

Griffyn began to blink heavily but paused as a group

of Dwellers stepped in front of him. They squealed a sharp noise that grated on his ears and forced him to take a step back. Three Dwellers jumped at him. They were faster than men, but their movements seemed to slow down. Swing the Masamune from the left.

Though he didn't understand it, he did as the voice in his head commanded. The Masamune slashed through the Dwellers as if they were nothing.

Duck.

He crouched as another dweller tossed itself from behind and fell flat on its face.

"Veda, if you are guiding me, then do not fail me." Griffyn prayed.

Onwards. Towards the giant.

Griffyn ran towards the giant. He scanned his surroundings as he breezed through the ranks of Dwellers who were torn into two halves. Kaven had split the soldiers into two flanks, and this created a gap in the middle.

As Griffyn approached the giant, he noticed a few Dwellers at the sides that were ready to attack him.

Don't stop. Keep moving.

Griffyn ignored them. Just before they attacked, soldiers appeared in front of them and put them to the sword. It was as if a symphony was being played. One that was elegant. As he went closer towards the giant, he felt the air become thicker, some residue of ash filled the oxygen that he breathed.

It was then that he stopped in his tracks. He lifted the Masamune and pointed it upwards. The thing stood at least a hundred feet tall. Griffyn couldn't even gaze upon its eyes.

"Here I stand," he said as he tried to catch his breath. "Come forth, and protect your Gods from me!"

The giant let out a war cry that generated enough force it almost imitated the Masamune. Griffyn was pushed back just by the sheer might of that force.

"God, you stink..." he noted as he struck the Masamune in the ground. He let out a cry as his sword glowed orange. "I will kill you all, you hear me!" he shouted as the giant halted.

The giant moved its arm backwards and swung it hard. Though its movement was slowed due to its size, the same couldn't be said about the damage that it was about to bestowed upon them.

Roll to the left. Quick!

"That's exactly where he is aiming!" Griffyn shouted but did so none the less. He managed to squeeze through just enough of a gap to avoid the calamity.

Don't let it swing again!

"How..." Griffyn growled.

"Who are you talking to?" Kaven asked as he approached.

"What are you doing here?"

"Look behind you!" Kaven shouted as he stepped in front of him. A quick glance was all Griffyn needed to notice that the battle had shifted. The force that the giant made had tipped the scale. Soldiers lost their footing, and Dwellers made quick work of those distracted.

"I'm trying..." Griffyn huffed, his face flushing in anger.

"Try harder! We've almost lost half our forces—" Kaven paused as the two of them began to feel a buildup of another swing coming their way.

To the left. Again!

Griffyn pushed Kaven to the left and rolled with him. They managed to escape its grasp once more. Kaven's eyes were wide. "How did you—"

"Shut up," Griffyn spat as he got up and faced the giant one more. "How do I do this? How do I bring him down?" Griffyn said as he kept his gaze fixed upon the giant. As it began to prepare for another swing, Griffyn let out a cry and swung the Masamune in the air as hard as he could.

There was a moment of silence. Then the Masamune glowed orange yet again, and a burst of wind from its steel collided with the giant. The collision sent waves across the area; the noise crackled into the sky. The giant lost its footing and began to descend on the ground.

Quickly now, jump on its body. Make haste.

Griffyn shook his head gently, and then ran towards

the giant that was in mid fall. He climbed up on its legs and continued straight towards its chest.

He screamed at the top of his lungs as he drove the Masamune into the giant's heart. The creature wailed in agony, but this one didn't have enough force to shatter the air. Life was fading away from it. Griffyn's brows rose as a big smile lit up his face.

You're not done. He has another heart, to the left.

"Two hearts?" Griffyn gawked for a moment, but then pulled the Masamune and shoved it to the left. The giant's cries turned wild as its body finally hit the ground with Griffyn atop its chest.

Griffyn's breath became short and a lump formed in his throat. Trying to take in as much air as his lungs would allow, he glanced back to see a shocked Kaven staring at him. He smiled and noticed all those on the battlefield, dweller and soldier alike, were looking at him.

Griffyn's eyes flashed back to Kaven and he pointed towards the soldiers with his brows. Then, he raised his sword to the bewildered soldiers. Their cries rose as the Dwellers let out a dumbfounded squeak in unison.

"Fall in line!" Kaven shouted as he stood up, readying to slay the last of the demons.

Griffyn jumped down from the giant's body and rushed to Kaven's side. "No, we should retreat. The battle is won, and now's our chance to—"

The earth rumbled at Griffyn's feet, stopping his

words in their tracks. Stones shook and soldiers quivered, but this time it was no giant that caused it. A dark and fluid discoloration formed on the ground next to Griffyn.

Dodge to the right.

"What?" Griffyn gasped as a moment passed, and he heard a shuttering noise. He pushed Kaven away and dodged just in time to miss the sword swing by a dweller that had appeared from beneath the fluid.

It wore armor that he recognized. It was their lord, the same Dweller that spoke to him in the camp. The one he pushed aside with the Masamune.

"What the hell?" Kaven gawked as he pointed his sword.

"No," Griffyn said to him as he eyed the Dweller Lord. "Came back to run away again like the coward you are?" he addressed.

The Dweller Lord let out a laugh. "I see your ego reached the sky in my absence, but I'll indulge. After all, it is my mistake for letting you live."

"The way I remember it, you tucked your tail and ran from me. I wouldn't say you let me live."

"And just because you survived, you became lord over them?" The Dweller Lord wondered as he pointed at Kaven and the rest of the soldiers.

Griffyn leaned towards Kaven. "I'll distract him. Retreat back inside and look for a signal."

"And what signal would that be?" Kaven said.

# TITANLORD

The Dweller Lord jumped towards Griffyn as he slashed that gleeful silver sword of his. Griffyn parried it with the Masamune. "Go! You'll know when you see it!" he demanded as he tried to exert as much pressure to hold off that thing.

"Remember what I told you before? When we first met?" the Dweller Lord said as a grin shaped on his face. His muscles tensed. "You are mortal, and all mortals tremble before us," he added as his dark and hollow eyes grew wider.

Griffyn struggled at the force of the dweller. He looked at Kaven from the corner of his eye. He needed to know if their plan was going well. The soldiers had covered Kaven, and they were moving at a steady pace back towards Wynne. The rest of the Dwellers were marching in unison now. They were much more organized than before.

"Dammit," he swore as sweat trickled at the back of his neck.

"You seem troubled. May I offer assistance?"

"By all means," Griffyn said as his tone broke. "Fall down on your sword and die, rid us all of your filth."

The Dweller Lord let out a laugh. "If only you were as good with the sword as you are in your defiance against the Gods," he said before he struck another time.

The force of the collision pushed Griffyn back. "Keep your mouth shut, now of all times..." he muttered under his breath. He wiped the sweat that beaded on his forehead with his left hand.

"Such a shame, to lose one with your potential. Prowess means little when faced with overwhelming strength," the Dweller Lord said as he took slow but paced steps towards Griffyn. "To think Veda called you the God Child... Is this truly humanity's best effort to survive?"

Griffyn's brows narrowed as he rushed in and swung to the left. The dweller dodged the strike and struck Griffyn's head with his elbow.

Griffyn coughed as his face went down to the ground. "You sack of wine!"

"A sack of wine? What insult is this?" the Dwellers face crept into a thin smile. "Do you see now how futile it is to stand against me?"

Griffyn scanned his surroundings yet again; the soldiers were being backed into a corner. "I... I'm not strong enough," Griffyn mumbled as he forced himself to stand.

The Dweller Lord smiled as he neared Griffyn and looked him in the eye. "At last, you begin to understand. Be a good boy and kneel, would you?"

Griffyn let out a sigh. "But maybe I don't have to be," he said with a smirk. He kept his gaze fixed on the Dweller Lord, and raised his brows. "You will drop your sword, and retreat now."

The facial expression of the Dweller Lord morphed into a blank slate. Then his eyes widened and veins popped on his forehead. He took a step closer and grabbed Griffyn by his neck and squeezed as hard as he could.

Griffyn struggled to free himself, but he couldn't muster any strength as he fell on his back, the dweller's hand still squeezing the life out of him. "You... dare try to compel me? Me!"

Griffyn flailed against the Dweller, but couldn't do much but smile.

"What's that smile on your face? You arrogant little wimp of a child. You smile even when you're about to perish alongside your race?" The dweller said as he seeped anger and breathed through his nose. "Why do you smile, boy?" he asked again as he eased his grasp on Griffyn's throat, enough so a bit of air could surge through his windpipe. "Answer me!"

"Look around..." Griffyn said.

The Dweller Lord lifted his gaze without letting go of his grip. His army laid in tatters. Wilson had come through at last and pushed them back. Together, they broke the demon army. The fighting was still going on, but it would be moments now before the entire demon army would be slayed to death.

"You think by killing them, you are doing yourself a favor? If one falls, another will rise in its place. All it would take is time," the Dweller Lord eased up. "This was your plan? Your grand attempt of defiance?"

"Who do you think they're coming for after they're

done?"

The Dweller Lord laid silent for a moment, and then, about twenty paces away, a beam of light shot from the ground. The grin found its way back to his lips. "Do you know what that is, boy?" he asked.

Griffyn swallowed as his eyes widened. "Nepherin..." he mumbled as he couldn't believe what he was witnessing. Nepherin, even amongst the Gods who descended, was called King. The single deity that had put everyone he held dear to the sword. Now, that calamity had befallen them again. Who would it be this time? Wilson? Kaven? Who next? Natasha? Will anyone survive this encounter? His thoughts haunted him.

"That look on your face," The Dweller Lord showed his teeth. "Allow it to sink in, the moment the realization comes upon you, that your doom is now certain."

Griffyn kept his gaze fixed on the light that stretched from the ground to the skies above. In the midst of it, Nepherin hovered as he defied all human laws.

"Gaze upon it. Go on, I'll allow it, the Light of the Divine!" the Dweller Lord said as he burst into laughter. "What do you feel? Tell me! Share with me this glorious—"

The Dweller Lord halted as he turned his head to look at Nepherin. The light that radiated broke and pulsed purple and then red before it completely cut off. Nepherin fell to the ground.

# TITANLORD

"What did you—"

Griffyn struck the Dweller Lord's chest with both of his feet, pushing him away. He rolled back up, picked the Masamune, and pointed it towards him. "Veda... any advice on how to handle this would be much appreciated..." Griffyn said under his breath.

Run.

Griffyn's eyes widened. Even more so when his gaze fell on the King of the Gods, who was drenched in sand. "He fell..." he mumbled, but then averted his gaze back to the Dweller Lord.

"Griffyn!" he heard Wilson and Kaven cry as they approached.

"Go back!" he shouted as he swung the Masamune in the direction of the Dweller Lord then turned and ran towards them. "Go back! We have to get out of this place right now!" Both of them did as he commanded as all the soldiers followed.

"Is that him?" Wilson asked as he fell into place beside Griffyn and kept running. "Is that one of the Gods?"

Griffyn continued running. "He's not a God, he's *the* God."

"Nepherin? *That's* Nepherin?" Kaven intercepted. "Why does he look so... pitiful?"

"I'm not sure. Something happened just now, something big, but we won't find out if we get slaughtered here," he warned as they reached the gate. They were surrounded by the remnants of the Red Hand's army and those part of Wilson's.

"Shut the gate!" Griffyn cried at the top of his lungs, and the soldiers happily obliged.

# CHAPTER 20

## *Killer of Gods*

Never so soon did the three of them agree on something as they scaled up the walls one more time to take a closer look at what happened. "I met one of them once. They somehow warped right inside our camp and interrupted us," Kaven said.

"And you of all people lived to tell the tale?" Wilson mocked.

"If it wasn't for the Red Hand, that thing would've decimated us on the spot. I understand why Griffyn thinks we must retreat."

Griffyn shook his head. "You don't understand." He took a deep breath as he kept his eyes fixed on Nepherin "We have to run. Run and never look back. Our best hope is to understand what took place here," he said as he turned and looked over the courtyard.

Wilson smirked at Griffyn, and then walked towards the edge. "We'll never make it outside like this. They will pursue us to the ends of the world if they keep their eyes on us."

"Regardless, we have to at least try to make it out alive," Kaven's brows narrowed. He knew that Wilson was up to something. "What are you—"

"Wait, what is that thing doing?" Wilson cried. His eyes widened, and his pupils dilated.

Griffyn came forth to take a look. Their jaws nearly hit the floor.

"Is that..." Kaven mumbled.

"Nepherin..." Griffyn added.

"What the hell does he think he's doing?" Wilson gasped as he took a few steps backwards. Kaven felt his heart beating. It raced for the first time in a while. He was a veteran general under the Red Hand. He had seen many atrocities, yet the one that laid dormant within his mind was not the one where the Red Hand had gained his nickname, but rather, it was that time when one of the Gods lesser than Nepherin had interrupted a meeting of generals.

He still remembered that sense of helplessness. Normal weaponry does not affect them, he remembered what Ben had said after everyone present attacked that thing in unison, to no avail. His beats twisted within his body. He tightened his hands into a fist. He placed one hand on his sword's hilt. A rattling noise rose.

"You're shaking?" Wilson said as he looked at him.

"Of all the things that I've seen in war, this, right here, terrifies me the most," he admitted as he tried to still his hand.

"They're not immortal," Griffyn broke his silence as the three of them gazed upon Nepherin.

He was walking. A squeak followed in his trail as the King of the Gods held his staff, dragging it along with him. His golden helmet covered his face and shone bright, even in broad daylight. He was emitting light. Yet, towards his forehead, something wasn't right.

Nepherin was walking. A King—no, a God—was using his feet to walk across a bloodied battlefield filled with demon and human bodies. Embers still remained lit, but as Nepherin neared them, they went out.

"His helmet, it's bent..." Wilson said as he squinted his eyes. "I thought nothing could damage those damn things," he added under his breath. He turned towards Griffyn. "Is such a thing possible?"

Griffyn shook his head. "Last I saw him, the Red Hand had no weapon against him. He gave me the Masamune and stayed behind..."

Kaven's eyes widened. "That sounds like him," Kaven said as he turned his back and scaled down the wall.

"Where are you going?" Wilson asked.

"Like I said, that thing terrifies me—"

"Now is not the time for you to be startled, we must—"

"I was in the siege of Ospis!" Kaven shouted, his voice broke and he gritted his teeth. "Before you utter another word, I would advise caution."

Wilson's mouth curved into a smile. "I didn't mean to insult, but death is upon us. Now of all times we must band together, traitors and soldiers."

Kaven struck his foot on the ground and stood still. "Call me traitor, one more time."

"Stop!" Griffyn shouted as he came between them. "If you two are all we have left, then let's take a moment to welcome death as it carries us all to our graves."

Kaven clicked his tongue. "We need to come up with a plan."

"Against a God? We can just hope to escape," Wilson said as he smirked. "It's as Griffyn said. You need to run, and run fast."

"Wilson..." Griffyn mumbled.

Wilson took a deep breath and looked at his hands. "I was rendered useless once, but not this time." Wilson smiled subtly, without alerting anyone. "But perhaps, I can be of use yet," he said as he turned towards Griffyn, taking a few steps and placing his hand on Griffyn's shoulder. "No one can deny now that you are our kind's best hope at battling these things."

"No," Griffyn shot back at him. His eyes spread fire.

"It's useless," he said as he turned around yet again. "I've already made up my mind," he added as he looked at Kaven. "Take the boy, and protect him at all costs. It is very clear why he must live."

Griffyn rushed towards Wilson and grabbed him by the chest. "You don't get to take the easy way out, you hear me? You don't get to die just yet," Griffyn said as he pushed him back.

A loud thud and Griffyn's world went black.

Kaven had struck the back of Griffyn's head, and as he fell towards the ground, Kaven caught him. Kaven held him as his eyes shifted towards Wilson. He took a deep breath. "I'll keep him safe. That I promise you."

"He's not going to be happy about this, you know. He will probably resent you for quite some time."

"Then I'll take comfort in the fact that he will be alive to do so," Kaven felt his heart weigh heavy. He couldn't help but smile. "You're a good man, Wilson."

Wilson nodded. "Towards the keep, turn right just before the entrance. The path will take you outside the eastern side of the village."

Kaven nodded and swallowed the lump in his throat. He turned around, and hoisted Griffyn onto his shoulders. "You know, we say this thing when we know that we are walking to our death."

"That light nonsense?"

Kaven cracked a laugh. "Yeah, it is meant to remind us that we are of the light that is fighting to save this world from itself. And that it is by that light that we will eventually fall and return to."

Wilson glanced at the ground for a moment and sighed. "Death comes to us all," he said as he took a pause. "It offers no reason, nor justification. Death is death. Be it in darkness or light."

"Nevertheless, you are as honorable as any man I respect," Kaven said as he closed his eyes for a moment. "Of the light, by the light," he recited as he kept walking. "Soldiers! On me!"

# CHAPTER 21

## *Citadel*

**G**riffyn woke from his slumber. His head was fuzzy, and his vision blurred. He felt his insides thunder within him, and he let out a pained cry as he held his head with his hands. He then paused and scanned his surroundings; he was back inside a tent.

It seemed to have a different style than the one he remembered though. He tried to force the images of what happened to come to him, but it didn't work.

"Wilson?" he cried as he sat up. "Kaven? Anyone?" he added as a chill went down his spine. He reached for his waist, and then moved his hands over his body. Glancing left and right, his gaze fell short. The air caught in his lungs. He exhaled and took a deep breath as he got up and stepped towards the Masamune. It was placed on a table in front of him.

There was a wooden jug with a cup. He reached for it and poured himself whatever liquid was inside. He pulled the chair and sat down, holding the cup with his right hand as he covered his face with his left.

A noise neared.

Kaven.

Griffyn closed his eyes, and then chugged the cup. He cringed at the taste as he took a big sip. He then placed the cup on the table and shrugged.

"It grows on you." He heard the man who entered the tent say.

Griffyn turned his head towards him. "Why?" he asked. His tone broke with a frown. Those words felt like knives to Kaven as he staggered and came closer.

He took a seat. "He told me you wouldn't take it well," he said, pouring himself a cup and chugging it down in one sip. "This is the best wine we have. Though, I never thought you, of all people, would partake."

"I tried it before. The taste is horrible, but—"

"But it numbs down that burning fire in your soul, doesn't it?" Kaven wondered as he kept his gaze fixed on Griffyn.

"More like it is so disgusting that it shifts my mind," Griffyn said, his brows narrowed. "Something was wrong, Kaven," he began as he took a deep breath. "When he first appeared, did you see the light? It broke! Something was

# TITANLORD

wrong...I—"

"You would've died."

"You don't know that," Griffyn shot him a cold stare. "I'm sick of all of you trying to protect me when I am much stronger than you. I hold the Titan Powers, not you! So, stop—"

Griffyn halted as Kaven struck the table with his fist. "Too many men have died for you!" Kaven paused. "You keep crying all the damn time that you are strong, yet your actions and your words scream weakness!" Kaven's breath came short. He sighed and took a deep breath and pulled back in his chair.

Griffyn's eyes glazed around him. It wasn't an easy thing to accept, him actually needing protection. He tried to think of something clever to say, but nothing came to his mind, not even with all the powers of the Voice.

"Tell me about him," he finally spoke.

"The Red Hand?"

Griffyn nodded.

Kaven took another deep breath. "We never truly understood most of his decisions, but he would always come through when we needed him the most. You know why he's called the Red Hand?"

"His hand would be tainted red with the blood of his enemies after battle."

Kaven smiled a bit. "That's what the rumors say," he

chuckled as he scratched his lower chin and settled. "It was during the battle of Ospis, the City of Thieves. Impossible to breach, or so it was said, until we marched upon them. Hidden in a maze of sands, and naturally guarded by its position, Ben instructed his best men to stand on the hills. When those in Ospis saw his tactic, they decided to face us head on-a costly mistake as that was exactly what Ben had counted on."

"That sounds... amazing. He anticipated what they would do?"

"That was why everyone was terrified of him. The moment that man made a single move, it was too late to stop him. Because chances were, he had already seen the end."

Griffyn's ears perked up. "How did you join him?"

Kaven's smile faded. "Ben saved my life. It's the same with almost everyone. Before, I was just a watchman on another continent called Snodia. Bandits had plagued our lands, and when a brigade attacked us, it wasn't the Magmars who came to our rescue, but that man who motivated us and demanded we fight. Everything I have today, I owe it to him."

Griffyn smiled gently. "He seemed like a man who would never turn away from battle."

"It won't be like this for long. Soon enough, we will depend on you, for many things. But for now, you have to be reasonable when it comes to these things. Retreat is sound strategy when you know you will lose."

"Sometimes we have to risk everything," Griffyn

fought.

Kaven narrowed his brows. "You are not Benjen," he said as he leaned closer to him. "Stop trying to be anyone but you. Since the dawn of time, those who imitated others have never truly accomplished anything worthwhile."

Griffyn lowered his gaze. "I'd like to be alone if you don't mind," his tone brooked no argument. He turned his face and lowered his head.

"Don't take it all out on yourself," Kaven said. He got up from the chair and placed a hand on Griffyn's shoulder. "Whatever it may be, it is us who choose what we die for. Never take that as surrender, nor pressure," he then started to walk towards the exit.

"That's just the thing with all of this," Griffyn said before he took a pause. "I wish others would stop dying on my behalf."

Kaven took a good long look at him, then exited the tent.

Griffyn pondered for a moment. "What am I supposed to do?" he pleaded as he wrapped his head between his hands and struck his forehead against the table.

You were right.

"Excuse me?" Griffyn said as he lifted his head. "What did you just say, you useless bastard?" he spat. He blinked but the world around him seemed to turn colors. A haze of blue dominated his surroundings.

Standing before him was a person he once saw in the

Citadel. "It was you? All along? Eskiban, Mayor of the Citadel? You were the bird that flew away? You are Veda?"

Veda nodded. "It matters not. We will speak of this later."

Griffyn shook his head. "And what do you want to talk about?" he asked as a grin flashed across his lips.

"Something was wrong. Nepherin's connection to the Divine has been rendered... obsolete."

Griffyn shot back in his chair. "Why didn't you say anything? Do you lot only lend me your power when I'm about to die?" He tightened his fists. "What about those I care about, huh? How am I supposed to save the world if all who aid me decide to throw their lives away?"

"You've much to learn about Titan Power. We lend you nothing. This... deformity you see, this is the true power of the Voice. In time, you won't need guidance."

"Then what is it, huh? What is the key to summoning Titan Power; not when it's only convenient to you?"

Silence.

"That's what I thought," Griffyn shook his head. "Would I have been able to kill Nepherin, without his... connection?"

"You would've died," Veda shot back at him. His eyes seemed lidless. He took a step closer. "Even with no connection to the Divine, Nepherin is dangerous. Cross paths with him while you're half prepared and you're done for."

"Then what's the solution? Do we keep running away?"

"You go to the Citadel."

"The Citadel?" Griffyn repeated as he scratched the back of his head. "What's there?"

"Long before the Creator breathed life upon us, he locked something away, right here on this very Earth. Something of Divine origins. That is the key to defeating the Gods and banishing them for good. That is the path to victory."

Griffyn shook his head. "What you're saying is madness."

Veda shook his head. "You mistake intent. Soon you'll have an army strong enough to defend the world you sought to protect when you left Palleria."

"There are two reasons why I can't go now," Griffyn said before he got up from the chair. "Fort Eldren is besieged, and I intend to go help lift it."

"You must—"

"Then, there's what you said to Wilson and I, to go somewhere else. Was that a mistake on your end?"

Veda stood silent for a moment. "We've set something in motion that will—"

Griffyn took a deep sigh. "What am I fighting for, Veda?"

Veda's eyes widened as his head tilted a bit. "You are

our only hope against the darkness. You alone must carry this burden, for I do not know what perils the Gods will put you through-their knowledge far surpasses ours."

"How do we even know that we are the light?"

Veda's face contorted in anger. "That's for the Creator to decide," he stated as he neared Griffyn and placed a hand on his shoulder. "Remember when we stood against Nepehrin? You are no boy. You are something much greater than that."

"You... called me 'The God Child'"

Veda hesitated for a moment, but then stood straight. "Don't misinterpret. All beings are his children. You possess the power to repel free will. That power can also be used to—"

"Command the dwellers..."

Veda smiled. "I promise you, a time will come when you and I, will discuss this at length," Veda paused for a moment. "Kaven approaches. You mustn't forget the role you have yet to play. You've seen proof. The Creator sides with you. With all my heart, I believe that you are the light."

Griffyn pondered for a moment. As Kaven entered, the blue hue evaporated into thin air, as if it had never been there in the first place.

"Griffyn, we march now."

# CHAPTER 22

## *The March*

riffyn strode through the camp alongside Kaven. He scanned dozens of faces of the soldiers he fought alongside with. He knew one thing: there was some sort of dispute amongst them.

"I forgot to ask, is the army intact?" Griffyn wondered. His eyes widened as they approached another tent set up on the outskirts of their camp.

"Why do you ask?" Kaven said as he strolled inside and paused. He signaled Griffyn to enter with a nod of his head.

"There was someone else with Dale, someone who was...leading them?"

Kaven's face twitched. "Edgar... smart boy, but he

slipped away when you showed up waving the Masamune around."

Griffyn pushed the flap aside and entered. The tent was mostly empty, save for a table in the middle that had a map on top. A few pieces of small wood pegs were on it.

"This is where we are now," Kaven said as he pointed towards the piece that centered the map. "If we intend to reach Fort Eldren in time, we have to take no pauses."

"We are unsure if the Fort still holds, General," one of the men gathered around the table said."

Kaven took a glance at him. "And you don't know just how stubborn the Second is. The Fort still holds."

Griffyn scratched the bottom of his chin and took a good look around him. They all were seasoned veterans; they have not only seen war but have lived it," he sighed.

Everyone halted for a moment, and Kaven leaned towards Griffyn. "Is this too boring for you?"

Griffyn nodded. "You said we'd march, yet here we are in this little tent," he stated without thinking. "If we need to move, then let's move. There's no point in dragging things along in favor of strategy."

Kaven lowered his head. "I would've assumed you of all people would know how important strategy is."

"Not when a siege needs to be stopped."

A ruckus erupted as the strategists began to debate amongst themselves. They had all seen what Griffyn could do; he was able to draw the Masamune's power, just like Benjen could.

"It seems simple, yes, but—" Kaven began.

"But nothing. We don't know the situation. We don't know what they're up against. Giants? Dwellers? Or Gods?" Griffyn fought as he knocked the figures off the map. "We won't know how to best address something we don't see."

"And what do you suggest we do?" a strategist shouted.

"We do what we said we would...March!"

"What about the traitor? Others slipped away along—"

"We will deal with them when it's time! We sit here and wonder how we would turn a situation we know nothing about, by enemies we defeated here..." Griffyn said as he paused and took a deep breath.

"He's right," Kaven interrupted. "Let's move out."

The debate finally ended, as the strategists went out one by one. It didn't take long before only the two remained. "Don't you have to yell at someone to prepare to march?"

"Is that what you really think I do all the time?" Kaven chuckled.

Griffyn smiled but remained silent.

"You're worried?"

"I've... seen far too much death recently."

Those words touched Kaven in a way he didn't imagine. That boy had gone through so much. Not only that, but the weight of the world was at stake. The actions of this youngling would decide the fate of so many.

"Natasha is strong, Griffyn," Kaven comforted as he balled his fists. "Far stronger than any of us would care to admit."

"Because she's a woman, leading men?"

Kaven shook his head. "Because we see something in her. And by admitting it, we somehow imagine ourselves lesser for it. We want to protect her, because the Commander did so first."

Griffyn tilted his head to the floor. "I've only always been around women, and they were some of the best warriors I've seen, but that doesn't change anything... in battle, a single distraction can lay waste to the strongest."

"That is why we proceed, when things seem dark, so that we honor their sacrifices," Kaven said. He walked towards Griffyn and placed a hand on his shoulder. "Let's get out of here."

# CHAPTER 23

## *Thunder*

It was almost dusk. Griffyn and Kaven rode ahead of the army that mobilized. The sound of the men and women marching resonated with Griffyn, he had almost gotten used to it. They were heading north towards The Towers; the tallest mountains on the Mainland that oversaw all the continent. It was said that someone with a sharp gaze may catch a glance of the Twin Islands.

The roads were parched; it was almost as if the fires at Wynne had echoed far across the Earth's surface. Though they were put out shortly, there was still one question that had festered in Griffyn's mind.

"There's something that I don't understand," Griffyn said and Kaven leaned his head back, carefully so that his grip on the reigns wouldn't shift.

"The light that was broken... the way Nepherin fell from the air... and then walked towards us..."

"You think he's vulnerable now? Is that it?"

"Maybe, it just seemed so... unbecoming."

"Suppose you're right, would you like us to turn around and head back to face him?"

Griffyn rolled his eyes and sighed. "That's not my point. Something happened, and I think it could be the key to winning this-"

"Perhaps that's the problem," Kaven said as he cracked his neck and shifted his gaze forward.

"What?" Griffyn asked.

"You're still looking at this as a war, and not what it is."

"And what would that be?"

"Annihilation," Kaven said as a chill went down his spine.

Griffyn opened his mouth, but no words would come out. He then shifted his gaze towards the horizon. "Do you smell something burning?" he asked.

Kaven sniffed as hard as he could. "It's faint, but it's there," he said as he glanced at Griffyn.

Griffyn nodded towards him, then Kaven lifted his hand high in the air. The entire army that marched behind them halted. They weren't deployed for battle and were stretched into narrow columns. Six men wide and almost a thousand long.

One of the captains rode towards Kaven and Griffyn. "Sir?" he questioned, waiting for the news on why the march was halted.

"Be quiet," Kaven demanded as he remained still. He could hear the breeze gently swaying against them. He had tremendous experience in the battlefield, and he learned a lesson when he was in the siege of Ospis, 'never underestimate anything, even a subtle noise.' It was what every general of the Red Hand had learned the hard way.

Kaven looked at Griffyn and raised his brows.

Griffyn took a deep breath and closed his eyes. For a moment, he traveled back in time, to that vision he saw earlier. He put himself on that same throne and imagined all the lords that knelt before him. "What should we do?" he asked under his breath. It was subtle, but the answer came to him.

Flanks.

He opened his eyes, with a glimmer of blue. He blinked and his face twisted into a frown. "Flanks..." he mumbled.

Kaven jumped down from his horse and quickly looked at the sides. It was a narrow path, but they were surrounded with tall trees and lush grass. It's perfect for an ambush, he thought to himself.

"Who am I kidding? What kind of bandits would attack a moving army?" he said.

Griffyn got down from his horse and joined him. "What if they're not attacking?" he said as he unsheathed the Masamune and stepped closer towards Kaven.

It was quiet, to the point where both men could hear their own breaths. Their heart beats remained calm and steady. At this point, both of them had seen far too much for the element of surprise to do any real damage.

Then, ruckus.

A voice tore the silence and ripped the air apart. It was screaming, of many men and women. Horrified and scared cries that echoed across the entire region.

"Steady!" Kaven shouted as the men next to them ran back to the ranks, shouting orders.

The columns of soldiers each faced the outskirts of the path, shields in front, and their swords at the ready for whatever was coming their way.

"Wait!" Griffyn shouted as he squinted his eyes. "These are not the cries of attackers," he said as he pulled away from formation and stepped closer towards the right side of the path.

"Griffyn! Fall back to formation!" Kaven shouted.

Griffyn saw as far as his eyes would allow him. And then, in the distance, he could make the shape of someone running as fast as he possibly could. The closer he got to Griffyn, the faster he became.

"Griffyn!" Kaven shouted as he tried to reach him.

The man fell in front of his feet, but Griffyn caught him before he hit the ground. He was drenched in blood. "What happened?" Griffyn tried to ask him, but the man wouldn't answer.

Within moments, the cries of men and women became silent. Then growls followed. "Dwellers," Griffyn said as he placed the man down and unsheathed the Masamune.

The growls got closer and closer, not a single dweller appearing in his vision, until suddenly, silence enveloped them.

"On your right!" Griffyn shouted as he lifted the Masamune and out of the woods, jumped one of them. Foul hideous beasts they were, their blackened skins rivaled the darkest of nights. Griffyn slashed it in half with his sword, and as if on cue, Dwellers came pouring out from the woods.

Griffyn took a step back and lifted his head. There were more than he could count, and they were all heading his way. His grip on the Masamune loosened as he gawked at the scene.

A memory came into his mind as if on default. In the tent, when he was so sure that the Creator was communicating with him and was about to revive Leah, he remembered what he had said and the promise he made. It was time for him to shoulder this responsibility.

He tightened his grip on the Masamune and thrusted

in their direction. The wave echoed out, knocking nearly all of the dwellers that were coming his way back. Some were plastered on the trees, while others evaporated. There were survivors, but they were knocked back a great distance.

"We need to fall back," he said as he turned and opened his mouth. His jaw nearly touched the ground at what he saw. There were dwellers attacking from all sides of the road.

The soldiers had made a wall of shields and were slowly pushing forward. Griffyn caught a glimpse of Kaven fighting at the back. "Kaven!" he shouted.

He was stuck on the other side of that wall of shields. "Run, kid! We'll catch up!"

Griffyn's eyes widened as he began to weigh his decisions. He knew that it was too tough to get back to the ranks. By doing so, how many lives would he be risking? He was tired... tired of having people die out of some misinformed belief that he was the one that would deliver them salvation.

He gritted his teeth as his brows narrowed. "No," he said as he began to rush towards the dwellers held up against the shields. "I refuse to run anymore!" he cried yet again as he ran closer towards them.

"No, you idiot..." Kaven shouted.

Griffyn lifted his sword in the air but paused as a roar tore the sky apart. The battlefield laid silent, and all shifted their gaze to the horizon.

Dark thick clouds began to form right above them. Thunder began to strike in a specific direction; it was coming from the other side of the woods. It was aiming at something, precise and accurate. It couldn't have been a coincidence. Griffyn turned and gave his back to the Dwellers. "Nepherin..." he uttered. "I know something is wrong with you, and that you are now vulnerable, and I will do it, but now is just—"

"Push!" Kaven let out a cry at the top of his lungs as the soldiers at the front backed away, and the second line of soldiers stepped in, blazing with their swords and cutting through the Dwellers.

An opening formed where Kaven was. "Get over here!"

Griffyn ran as fast as he could and reunited with Kaven. He placed both of his hands on his knees and tried to catch his breath as best he could.

"Shields!" Kaven cried, and the soldiers exchanged lines again. He had used this opportunity wisely; the Dwellers were being pushed back.

"We need to retreat," Kaven said as he grabbed Griffyn. "Why did you break formation?" He shook him.

"Because I wanted to push them back..."

"Well, did you? Did you get all of them?" Kaven said as they both got startled at the sound of a loud clash. The soldiers continued pushing the Dwellers back.

"We can still win this," Griffyn fought.

"There is no winning this. We retreat, regroup and then try again to make it in time to break the siege."

Griffyn shook his head. "There isn't enough time."

Kaven turned and grabbed the back of his head with both of his hands. He then looked at Griffyn and pointed in the opposite direction. "We're not far from the Citadel. We left a garrison there led by Gilkas; he can help us."

"The... Citadel?" Griffyn repeated as he took a few steps ahead. He scratched the back of his head. "I think... we were supposed to go there instead."

"Great, since your highness agrees, then we head back to the Citadel and figure out what to do from there," he said as he stepped forward. "Soldiers!" he shouted.

"Wait!" Griffyn interrupted as he placed a hand on his shoulder.

"No, you have done enough damage already."

Griffyn pulled him back. "Hear me out, and then make the decision yourself."

Kaven stared into Griffyn's eyes. There was something different about him this time. It was almost as if he knew what was going to happen next.

"Instead of a regulated retreat, we give ground," he stepped forward and took a good look at the soldiers. "We will save more lives this way."

Kaven blanked. "That's a sound strategy. Good on

you," he said as he stepped closer to the soldiers. "Give ground!" he shouted. "One pace at a time, but do not falter!" he added as he took out his sword and tilted it towards Griffyn. "Stay here."

*  *  *

Kaven ran to the back of the lines. As the soldiers saw him a fire rekindled in their hearts, and they began to cheer loudly.

"Strike hard and true," Kaven encouraged as he patted the soldier on the front line and exchanged places with him. Kaven swung his sword at the beasts again and again, but against the Dwellers who relied only on numbers, this would only hold them for so long.

"Push!" Kaven shouted as the soldiers around him pulled back. The second line came to the front and blasted the Dwellers with their shields.

"Now, give ground!" Kaven shouted, and the second line retreated by three steps, then the lines exchanged again. Kaven was at the back once more with Griffyn.

"This will take a bit," Griffyn said to him.

"You're right, but we will save many lives," Kaven explained as he glanced at Griffyn's hand, which laid on the Masamune's hilt. "Don't, sometimes, order greatly surpasses power."

"I..." he uttered. "I made a mistake earlier, I apologize."

Kaven shook his head. "Now isn't the time for this, save it. So long as you learn from every mistake you make, then you're making progress."

"We don't need progress... we need a resolution, and quickly too."

Kaven looked in his eyes and took a sigh. "I know this must be difficult for you, but we, right now, are all that stands against all of this."

"I guess I somehow forgot that we are at the forefront of this war," Griffyn admitted and balled his hand into a fist. He took a hard look at it, his skin looking to have aged more than his actual years. "But what of the innocent? What of the average person trying to live their normal life? What must they be thinking right now?"

Kaven lowered his head. "I sometimes forget that wars impact us all," he said. He took a deep breath. "Well, we must end this war as fast as we can, because only then can you look them in the eye and not fret their reaction."

Griffyn glanced to the back of the army. They were off the main road now. It was only a few hours to the Citadel, but it would take them a longer than anticipated to arrive safely.

# CHAPTER 24

## *Prophecy*

The sun was almost set. Griffyn and Kaven were leading the men against the Dweller horde that had come. They were struggling, but their casualties were at a minimum-a much needed change after so long and so much loss.

"We're almost there!" Kaven shouted to Griffyn who stood next to him.

The Citadel came into view, and shortly after exchanging lines, the Dwellers broke away from their attacks. They turned and began running to the other side.

"What just happened?" Griffyn gawked as the soldiers cheered briefly at the retreat.

"I'm not sure, but I'm grateful nevertheless," Kaven looked at the soldiers who were gasping for air. The battle took a heavy toll on them.

"We repelled them," Griffyn said.

"Either that, or we just played right into their hands," Kaven furrowed his brows and turned around. "Make haste to the Citadel. You'll have plenty of time to rest..." Kaven paused with a sigh. "Behind the comfort of its walls, and a familiar ugly face."

\* \* \*

It wasn't long before Griffyn, along with Kaven, reached the Citadel. The gate seemed rusty, but the place was secured. The banners of the Red Hand flew across it.

"That's a familiar sight," Griffyn sighed as they both took a few steps closer. A screeching sound followed. However uncomfortable for the ears, it was a welcomed change against the sound of battle.

"Wait till you meet him," Kaven said before he turned his head to face him. "Let me do the talking, okay?"

Griffyn nodded.

A man walked towards them from inside the gate, flanked by guards. He was bald and well built; his muscles were tensed. The closer he got, the more Griffyn realized the difference of height between them.

"Why is this worm holding a sword bigger than his dick?" the man said as he shot a glare at Kaven.

"Hello, Gilkas. It's wonderful to see you here again," Kaven said as he went to embrace the man.

Before Kaven closed the distance between them, Gilkas drew his axe and threw it as hard as he could against the ground. "Answer the question, Holt."

Kaven paused as his gaze shifted. "This... worm right here," he said as he pointed towards Griffyn, "he's the one the Commander entrusted to bring his sword."

Gilkas gasped, his eyes widening.

"There's much to discuss, but for now, we need rest—"

"You still haven't answered my question, Holt," Gilkas demanded as he grabbed his axe and pulled it out of the ground.

"Kaven, let me—"

"Wait," Kaven interrupted Griffyn. He placed a hand on his chest. "Gilkas is proud, but he has always been loyal. Surely, he understands the ratifications that would ensue should he take one swing at you."

"Last I saw you, the Commander took you and all of our forces out of here. And now you return with less than half the numbers and a little shit in place of him. How would you expect me to take that?"

"I would expect you to know your place and shut your mouth," Kaven warned as he looked him in the eye. "Now fall in line, Captain," he added, his gaze still fixed on him.

Gilkas scratched the back of his head. "General..." he

uttered before a smile appeared from ear to ear. "What the fuck have you been up to?" he added as his guard went down and he embraced Kaven.

Kaven squeezed gently, then pushed him back. "We're not kids anymore, remember?" Kaven said as he returned the smile.

"What is even going on here?" Griffyn asked, his brows furrowing together in confusion.

"You," Gilkas addressed, pointing in his direction. "That is still one giant sword. But if the General is fine with it, then I guess you're the one the Commander was waiting for."

Griffyn squinted at him. "What do you mean?"

"I said not here, Gilkas. Let's get inside." Kaven said as he waved his hand and the army mobilized again.

"Fine. But General, we need to talk right away."

Kaven nodded and the three of them marched inside and through the gates.

The Citadel was quiet. The narrow path that led to the keep remained untouched. Guards were stationed on the wall even at this time of night. "Are you expecting an attack?" Griffyn wondered.

"Sharp, this one," Gilkas said before he nodded. "Things haven't been that stable since we took the city. The old had reminisced about their fucking mayor at every turn."

"How did the Commander deal with that?" Kaven

asked.

"He didn't have to. As soon as we entered, the Commander abolished their debts, and that seemed to make things more stable here, aside from a few zealots."

"Zealots?" Griffyn jumped in.

"The Spymaster was charged with treason. The Commander tried really hard to pardon him, but he was bent on challenging him to a fight."

"That makes no sense. Ben would never bite," Kaven said.

"True, but he was left with no choice. That son of a whore managed to get the best of Clint."

"Clint is dead?" Griffyn asked then paused. He scanned his surroundings and took a good look at the market district to his right. It seemed peaceful enough. Last he was here, he was with Vendel and Rory...they had helped push back the first Dweller invasion. He would never forget that day.

Gilkas and Kaven turned towards him. "Not here. Let's keep walking," Kaven said to Griffyn before he took a few steps closer and placed a hand on his shoulder. "In war, there are always casualties. But remember through their sacrifice, we add to our own fight."

"But... you knew him?" Griffyn asked.

"It was during the first rebellion. Clint Sebastian was a captain fighting alongside us," Gilkas explained to him. "One day, Kaven will tell you all about it."

Griffyn gawked for a moment, then regained his composer. "I have way too many questions to ask on the streets. Let's move fast."

Kaven took a deep sigh and resumed walking. The keep came into view then; a grand structure made of marble that stood tall, almost as high as the walls.

Gilkas pushed the gates open, and guards saluted him. They walked through the corridor and passed by the inner chambers, where the Red Hand once lived after he had conquered the Citadel.

They reached the private chambers, and Gilkas opened the door. The room was clean and without a speck of dust. There was a table with four chairs at its center.

Kaven took the closest seat then gestured at the others. "Sit down," he asked, and the rest followed. Kaven took a breath. Here sat the Commander in his final moments... what was it that he saw? he thought.

"First things first," Gilkas said as he took a deep breath. "I think the Commander knew that he wouldn't return here. I had a feeling that I didn't want to believe, but alas, this twat sits in front of me, with that sword."

"Okay, my name is Griffyn. Not twat, not little worm, not whatever it is you want to say. It is Griffyn," he shot him a cold look.

"When we were here last, the Commander insisted to leave you, to guard something so to speak," Kaven said, bringing the conversation back around.

"Yes. His last words to me were 'the Citadel must not fall,' and I wish that he hadn't trusted me this much, but..." Gilkas admitted.

"If that's the case, then it's fair to say that he had a pretty good idea of what was going on," Griffyn scratched the bottom of his chin. "Do you know if he had any...weird dreams? Or heard voices?"

Kaven and Gilkas both gawked at his odd questions. Gilkas gawked. "Why is that relevant?"

"I don't know yet, but I've been having some thoughts towards the nature of the Gods. I am almost confident that something important has happened. For some reason, ever since that light broke, he has seemed more...mortal."

Gilkas widened his eyes and glanced at Kaven.

"Don't ask," Kaven replied.

"So, what's the plan then? You retreated here to rest, and then what? Are we heading out to face off against that Nepherin thing?" Gilkas asked.

Kaven shook his head. "Fort Eldren is besieged. As we speak, Natasha is holding them off. We are heading out next thing in the morning to relieve them. Once we are reunited, then will we know what to do next."

"Eldren is besieged? The Commander is dead...what more news do you two bring?" Gilkas wondered before he got up from his chair. "Sleep. We will speak in the morning."

"Where are you going?" Griffyn asked.

"To get things in order," he replied, shutting the door behind him, leaving Griffyn and Kaven to discuss.

"Was that too much information?" Griffyn pondered.

Kaven shook his head. "We haven't the time to spare," he said before he too got up. "Why do you think Ben said the Citadel must not be lost?"

"I'm not sure, honestly. Ben was terribly intelligent, and he had Titan Power, so to ignore his commands so soon would not be advisable."

"Then sleep. Tomorrow we will uncover whatever it is he left us here," Kaven said as he took a good look at his hands. "Maybe the day that we force his sword down Nepherin's throat will come sooner rather than later."

Griffyn stood. "I would caution against that," he sighed. "We don't have time to lose, Kaven. So tomorrow morning, you head out with the army, and I'll catch up to you, along with Gilkas."

Kaven looked at Griffyn. "You have a point."

"This is the next best move. Whatever it is that Ben left for us to find, I'll get it and come straight your way. With luck, I'll manage to catch up before you reach the fort."

"Do you... have the dreams too?" Kaven asked. His thoughts oozed back and forth deep within his mind. "The truth is Ben would often wake up drenched in sweat."

Griffyn's brows narrowed. "Did he ever share anything about them?"

Kaven shook his head. "He always kept those things close to his chest."

Griffyn smiled, and then walked towards him. He placed his hand on Kaven's shoulder. "I want you to know that it wasn't because he didn't trust you or that he thought you wouldn't understand."

Kaven feigned a smile.

"It's heavy, you know... the burden of being the one with the Masamune. It's not something that comes easily."

"With every passing moment you begin to behave and sound more like him, and I'm not sure that's a good thing," he chuckled lightly.

Griffyn leaned closer. "Mine is heavier than his was, Kaven."

Kaven turned his head towards him and frowned.

"I have the task of not only prevailing, but in also making sure that Ben, Rory, and Vendel didn't all die in vain," he admitted as he walked back and sat on the chair again. He spent a good minute looking at his fist.

"Can you do it?" Kaven asked as he tilted his head.

"Hm?"

"Can you actually do it? Can you help deliver us from the darkness in his place?"

Griffyn pondered it for a moment, then sighed. "It's not about darkness or light... life in actuality is pretty pointless. Whatever side you're on —be it light or darkness—doesn't matter if you are shredded and crushed by Nepherin in the end."

Kaven scratched the back of his neck. "Meaning?"

Griffyn shook his head. "What does it matter if we're light or dark in this very instance? Will it change the purpose of our fight? Or will it just cement our desire to live?" he said before he took a deep breath. "The more I think about it, the more it makes sense," he lifted his head and pushed his hair aside. "It's all the same."

Kaven took in whatever air his lungs could muster. He knew that a peaceful sleep would not come so easily after this day. "Get some rest, C... comrade," he said as he finished, he bowled his face and closed his eyes as hard as he could.

"I'll see you soon, brother," Griffyn replied.

# CHAPTER 25

## *The Sword of Light*

**G**riffyn opened his eyes lazily, his vision seemed blurry and almost fazed. He tried to get up, but his movement was hindered. The Masamune was in his hand. He shifted his weight and blinked a few times to clear his sight.

"Well? What do you make of it?"

"Veda..." Griffyn mumbled before trying to sit up once more. He still felt heavy, as if he wasn't meant to awaken. "What do I make of what?" he groaned.

"This was where I used to sleep."

"Right," Griffyn sighed. "I forgot you were once the mayor of this Citadel. What do you want?" Griffyn asked.

Veda appeared unfazed; he didn't shift his gaze nor his position. "Me?" he paused and sighed. "I want nothing."

"Then why this?" Griffyn gestured to his immobilized state.

"I'm not doing this, Griffyn. You are."

Griffyn narrowed his brows and squinted. "What are you saying?"

"There's another amongst us. Someone who has ties to you. Someone you wish was there for you but isn't."

A figure was walking behind Veda. The footsteps each echoed in his ears, ringing clearly. The posture and the composure, the way the person moved was full of pride.

"Who's there?" Griffyn asked. Veda was no longer anywhere to be seen.

"It's about time we met under lighter circumstances," he heard the figure say. The figure stepped into the light, his hands entwined behind his back and his face all too familiar.

"Benjen!" Griffyn gasped as he tried to move again but couldn't.

"Save your energy, young one. You're going to need it very soon."

"Are you really here?"

Benjen shook his head and lifted his brows.

"Is this... Titan Power?"

Benjen shook his head again. "To do something like this requires a bit more than the Titans aiding you. Lucky for us, you aren't just a Titan anymore."

Griffyn's brows narrowed again. "Veda kept calling me the God Child... It seems I can compel others to do things they otherwise wouldn't do. Is it somehow linked to this?"

"So many questions, and so little time," Benjen said as he took a few steps closer. "Don't try to be anybody else besides yourself. That is why I left you the sword."

"I can't, Ben... I'm not you. I can't lead anyone, and I sure as hell can't beat Nepherin." Griffyn admitted, tears entering his eyes.

Benjen shook his head and sat on the bed next to Griffyn. He placed his hand on his chest. "Do you hear your heartbeats? That is how confident I am in my decision. I believed in you back then. Now it is time for you to believe in yourself."

Griffyn tried to speak but couldn't as his head became fuzzy. More than anything, he needed some form of guidance. Now that the Red Hand himself was before him, he finally knew that he wasn't going to get any answers.

"For a long time, I needed some form of hint that I was heading in the right direction. I keep trying to imagine what you would do, but I don't think I know you well enough...I'm supposed to be the light that purges the darkness, but I am just so... lost."

"You were never meant to be anything," the words parted Ben's lips as he shrugged.

Griffyn tilted his head. "What am I? Huh, Ben? If there is anyone who can answer me, truthfully, it's you. It's your words I trust, not Veda, not Kaven, not anyone else."

Ben exhaled. "You were never meant to act, Griffyn. You were there just as a failsafe."

Griffyn's eyes widened.

"All the way south, beyond The Shred, lies the Twin Islands and Hollow Land. Legends speak of Brelleck, an ancient Titan who separated them with his fist."

"Brelleck?"

Ben nodded. "That same legend states that he did this after he learned of the Grand Design, in protest. Because what had to come seemed so vile to him that he took it as an offense to attribute it to the Divine."

"What was it?" Griffyn asked.

"That a time of great evil will come upon the lands. Darkness will have nearly swallowed all, children will grow without fathers, their mothers will forsake them, and blood will pour from cities and fill rivers."

"That seems... too ominous for a prophecy."

Ben smiled. "It is, but it also says that the Creator will shine a light to pierce through it, should it ever come it."

"And you think I'm the light that was promised?"

Ben stood, looming over Griffyn, and placed both of his hands on his shoulders. "Not just any light, Griffyn, but his light," he said, then took a deep breath.

# TITANLORD

"What does that mean?"

Ben shook his head and smiled again. "Be the storm that this world needs, Griffyn, be the storm."

# CHAPTER 26

## *Filius*

Kaven strolled through a long corridor. It was morning, the smell of marble never seemed to waver against the flow of time. There were paintings on his left and right, but aside from a glare or two, he didn't stop until he was in front of the door.

"You're awake."

Kaven turned his head towards Gilkas who had marched straight there as well. Kaven yawned. "We haven't the time to sleep. We have a siege to lift. Are you ready?"

Gilkas cracked his knuckles and neck. "As ready as I'll ever be," he said and pointed with his brows at the door. "Wake him up and join me in the catacombs."

"Gilkas..."

"This is important," Gilkas interrupted before walking away.

Kaven clicked with his tongue and then knocked.

"Come in."

Kaven opened the door. He saw Griffyn standing far from the table, facing the wall with the Masamune ready at his hip. "You slept well?" he asked.

Griffyn turned. "As well as the likes of us deserve," he said with a smile. "Are we ready to head out?"

Kaven shook his head. "Gilkas is waiting for us in the catacombs. He says it's important, but I..."

"Then let's hurry down there and see it through," Griffyn interrupted as he walked past Kaven.

As the two stepped out into the hallway, a roar shook the grounds beneath them causing them to freeze in their tracks. Everything around them moved against its will.

"What was that?"

"Thunder," Kaven said as he gazed outside the window. "Come, we haven't the time to lollygag."

Together, they made their way towards the catacombs. They walked through the halls until they reached a heavily reinforced wall. Griffyn pushed the door open, and a rattling noise overtook their ears.

A piercing light bulged against the darkness as the

staircase became illuminated. "It's down here," Griffyn said as he picked up the torch that hung on the wall to his right.

"You've been here before?" Kaven asked, his brows narrowed, but Griffyn didn't answer. The silence was deafening to the point where they could hear their own hearts beating in their chests. "Why is it so dark?"

"The dead lay here. I believe it's safe to assume that they prefer it over light," Griffyn explained, his gaze never shifting.

Kaven turned towards him and shook his head.

"You're late." Gilkas' voice echoed from the darkness.

"We're here, aren't we?" Kaven answered as Gilkas stepped into the light radiating from Griffyn's torch. "What do you want to show us?" he asked.

Gilkas gritted his teeth. "This way," he said as he turned around and tilted his head forward.

"Well, let's not wait any further, shall we?" Griffyn said impatiently.

Gilkas nodded and led the way ahead. "After you all left, I began exploring every inch of this hole," he added as he glanced at Kaven. The memories of him leaving along with Ben were still vivid in his mind.

It was his right thigh that has been pierced by a sword. He pleaded with Ben to let him leave with them, but he wouldn't have it. "The Citadel must not be lost," Gilkas sighed. "That's what the Commander's final words were to me. At first, I thought he was being kind, as to not wound my pride, but it seems that he was up to something."

"Haven't you heard something like that from the Voice?" Kaven asked, shifting his gaze towards Griffyn.

Griffyn nodded. "At every point since I made it out of the Capital. The Voice has been consistent in one thing, and one thing only: I have to visit the Citadel."

"And you hardly mentioned anything about it." Kaven huffed.

"It's not exact. For example, when we were discussing how to approach the Wynne situation, the Voice insisted we explore south. Sometime later, we learned that a zealot army had gathered there."

Kaven paused and turned. "And you did what?"

"Nothing. We didn't really have enough time to recoup anything. The second we were inside, remember, the soldier that came warning us about the Dwellers?"

"Was he one of the scouts you sent?"

Griffyn nodded. "It speaks to reason that the Dwellers had made quick work of the zealots first. In fact, I'm guessing that is the sole reason why we emerged in one piece... well, almost, anyway."

"You two done with your chit-chat?" Gilkas interrupted.

Kaven and Griffyn looked at each other and shrugged

their shoulders. "You brought us all this way to show us a dead end?" Kaven shot at him, crossing his arms.

"Light," Gilkas said. He extended his hand towards the torch that Griffyn held. "Come on, we haven't got all day."

Griffyn shook his head and took a few steps forward. He raised his hands against the wall that was covered under the guise of darkness. After a few moments scanning it, a stone tablet appeared. "What is this?"

"It's durable, this one. I tried to force it open with many tools, but the damn thing is as hard as steel. I figured whatever the Commander wanted is on the other side of this wall."

There was a shape engraved in the tablet. It was the image of a young man who held a tree branch. His body seemed exposed save for the waist. A circular shape towered above his head.

"What makes you think there is another side to this," Kaven asked as he stepped a bit closer. "The detailing is marvelous." He gently touched the tablet.

As his fingers grazed the stone, a sharp grating noise erupted from the wall. The ground beneath them shook, and the tablet began to glow. "What the hell..." Kaven gasped.

"It's never done that before," Gilkas said before he took a pause. "Are these... holes?"

The air around them thickened, and a burst of energy

came out of the tablet. The energy oozed, the glow flowing out and around them. It reached Griffyn, and suddenly stopped.

Griffyn caught his breath. He looked to his left and right, but nothing seemed to be moving. Kaven and Gilkas included. It was as if they were frozen in time. Griffyn tried to move, but felt compelled not to. "What is this..." he mumbled, then he shut his eyes.

He could see something amidst the darkness behind his closed eyes. It was faded, but he could make out the details of Fort Eldren. Dwellers were crawling everywhere. His vision tunneled as he went through the gates and towards the Keep, then inside. That's when he saw him, the Dweller Lord, sitting atop the throne.

Red tainted the grey stone at his feet, blood dripped from the walls around him. His vision tilted to the side and he saw Natasha on the floor, not moving. His vision then shifted to the other side of the room, as the doors to the Keep opened. There he stood, alongside Kaven.

His eyes shot open then. He gasped for air, as if his head had been shoved under water. He scanned his surroundings and saw Gilkas and Kaven standing in front of him.

"Are you okay?" Kaven worried as he placed a hand on his shoulder. "What happened? What's wrong?"

"I'm fine," Griffyn uttered as he slowly turned his head towards the tablet. A blue and orange light ebbed from it. "I'll be damned..." he mumbled.

"What's going on, boy?" Gilkas asked, taking a few steps back. He eyes fixated on the tablet. "I've never seen anything like this before in my entire life," his tone shook.

Griffyn turned to Kaven. "Listen, you need to leave."

"Pardon?" Kaven leaned closer, raising a brow.

Griffyn turned towards him and placed a hand on his shoulder. "I ask that you place your trust in me, as did Ben when he held the Masamune."

Kaven stepped back, taking careful steady breaths. "Why?"

"I don't have time to explain, but if you leave right now, you might be able to stop it," Griffyn warned. He took a few steps towards the tablet and unsheathed the Masamune. "Go, take the army, and leave right now!"

Kaven didn't move, his brows furrowing. Deep within his heart, he knew Griffyn was serious and that he had seen something that neither Gilkas or him had. But he, too, wanted to know what was behind the door. "What about-"

"I'll be right behind you. I'll take care of this and will head out to meet you before you reach the Fort," Griffyn interrupted.

Kaven frowned. Of course, he knew the feeling of disappointment all too well, but it still stung his heart a little. Scratching his right ear, he looked at Gilkas and smiled.

"Don't be late," Kaven said as he turned around and made his way back.

Griffyn waved his left hand against the tablet, which had begun to pulse at his touch. "Step back," he said to Gilkas and nodded.

He raised the Masamune. The holes in its hilt began to react to the pulse. It was first blue, then orange, and then nothing. It lagged for a moment before it began the loop again. "Veda, Pollus, and Magnus," he said, looking at the Masamune.

"What is going on?" Gilkas asked, his heart coming faster at the unknown.

"It seems that this is a lock that was placed by the mayor. I think it needs all three holes on the sword to be filled before opening," he answered.

"Three holes?"

Griffyn widened his grip and turned the Masamune towards Gilkas. "See these? One for each Titan Power. Ben had the Strength, and now I have the Voice."

"So... we're missing what?"

"The Dream...Magnus, if I'm not mistaken. Nepherin has already taken him out."

"So whatever secret lays on the other side of this wall, the one the Commander gave his life to defend, the one thing that is meant to turn the tide to our favor is... locked, and we can't get to it because one of the Titans has been killed?"

Griffyn nodded. "Normally, yes."

"Normally?"

Griffyn scratched the bottom of his chin. "Veda, Pollus, Magnus. It's clear that it requires three Titans to open, but I'm hoping I can fill that gap," he explained before returning his eyes to the tablet.

"What?"

"Veda, Pollus," he repeated before pausing. He took a sigh. "Filius..."

The pulsing stopped. "Something... is happening," Gilkas said as he took a few steps backwards.

Griffyn looked into the eyes of the man on the tablet. "Open," he demanded, and the eyes glowed a light purple. The tablet pushed itself back.

A crackling noise grew louder as the markings glowed on the tablet, before slowly reducing to a pile of dust.

"Let's move," Griffyn said as he took the first few steps. Silence enveloped them once more as they delved further. Over time, he had learned to cherish the silence, but at that stage, it was growing into something that he never felt imaginable; he found comfort and peace within the distilled quiet. It wasn't long before the path ended, and against the wall laid a chest covered in dust.

"What is this?" Gilkas gawked.

The closer Griffyn got to the chest, the more a light seemed to be coming out of it. He placed his hand on its top. "It's warm," he muttered before opening it. The first thing he noticed was a scroll. He grabbed it and rolled it out.

"It's like the scroll the Commander had..." Gilkas gasped as he stepped closer and looked at it. "What does it say?"

The writings didn't make sense. It wasn't a language that Griffyn had ever seen before, but for some reason he sensed as though the letter was directly talking to him... or about him.

He closed his eyes for a moment and read it:

*Hail, Divi Filius.*

*If you are reading this, then times have changed. I wrote this to you so that you might understand the true purpose of your role in the Grand Plan. A thing, which your father has started, lays in jeopardy. I swore an oath that I would uphold His true vision, but the balance was tipped; I had to intervene.*

*By invoking the Sacrilegious, the children are now cut off from the Divine. They no longer possess the Well. They will fight as did the Titans before them, but at least you have a fighting chance.*

*Make haste, Filius, for a long night approaches, and it is only you that can separate fact from fiction. Strike hard and true.*

*Signed,
A friend.*

"Well, can you read it?" Gilkas asked.

Griffyn pondered the message for a moment before answering. *Just what do I tell him? And what the hell does this even mean?* he thought to himself. "During the battle of Wynne, Nepherin levitated in mid-air in the glow of a great white light. Then, almost suddenly, that light broke; effectively turning the battle around. It gave us the opportunity to retreat, but even then, Nepherin hadn't done anything like that before. He walked... Gilkas. He walked and dragged his weapon against the ground as any mortal would have."

"What do you mean?"

He tightened his grip on the scroll. "Their connection to the Divine is severed."

"Wait, you're actually saying we can kill the bastards?"

Griffyn turned and faced Gilkas, his eyes stern. "What if, thousands of years ago, Titans were the same as the Gods are now? But their connection was also severed?"

"You're speaking nonsense, boy."

Griffyn shook his head. "I'm betting that whatever Ben

was after, someone already got it. They used the only weapon against the Gods that can even the playing field, and they did it precisely when we were about to be quelled."

"A guardian angel?"

"Of some sort... that's my best bet anyway."

Gilkas grabbed his tunic and pressed him against the wall. "I don't know how many times now, but the only ones who call the Commander by his first and shortened name are ones he considers friends."

"I didn't mean..."

"Last night, you asked if he ever had weird dreams? Every night we would rush to him amidst screams, fearing that assassins had somehow got by us, only to find him battling his mind. You tell me, what should I be thinking?"

"Do you hate the fact that he entrusted me with his sword and message and not you? Or do you just hate that I seem to know more about him than you, after serving for I don't know how long under him?"

Gilkas gritted his teeth and took a deep sigh. His brows narrowed, and his face seemed to shake a bit. He let Griffyn go and stepped back. "None of us hate the fact that he chose you as his successor. None," he said as he turned around. "We stopped doubting him a long time ago; if he gave you the sword, you're the right person to have it. There's nothing more to it."

"Then the latter is true..."

"You talk like him, you think like him... I haven't seen you fight, but I'm guessing you fight like him as well."

"I honestly wouldn't know, but I'm not the great fighter that he was. Of that I'm certain."

Gilkas sat on the ground, a wave of exhaustion overtaking him. "Would you mind telling me how he died?"

Griffyn pondered for a moment. He was taken back at the request, but he realized that he had never told the full story. "He came in the nick of time. Too late to save Rory, but he saved me and my friend. He pushed Nepherin and the other God back. I've never seen anyone fight like him."

"What did it?"

"He got distracted."

"That's impossible."

"It's true," Griffyn sighed as he took a few steps closer towards him. "I was so mesmerized by the battle that I forgot he was doing all of this to save us. The moment he tried to warn me, to tell me to run, they got him. That's when he gave me his sword and took Rory's instead."

The silence that followed his words was deafening. He could hear gasps coming from the ferocious looking warrior who sat on the ground, listening to how his commander was killed in battle.

"That sounds like him, though, him dying is uncharacteristic. So, it must've been something unexpected that got him killed," Gilkas said as he stood. He wiped his face and looked at Griffyn. "Well, what do you want me to do?"

Something about those words struck Griffyn. Before him, laid one of the strongest warriors at the Red Hand's disposal, and he was asking him what to do. This was the only reality Griffyn knew now. "Stay here. The Citadel is important. In case whoever took whatever's in this chest returns, bring them to us."

Gilkas nodded. "What are you going to do?"

"Me?" Griffyn shrugged his shoulders and turned his back to Gilkas, "I have a siege to lift."

# CHAPTER 27

## *A Storm*

Griffyn had his gaze fixed on the gates of the Citadel. He was still inside, and something within him was boiling. He merely stood there in silence, against the sound of thunder tearing the skies apart.

"The storm should settle soon," one of the soldiers said to him.

"It's been three hours," he shot back.

"It's far better to wait for more favorable weather than to go in and risk everything..."

Griffyn turned and looked at him. "And what exactly would I be risking? As we speak, Kaven is already on his way towards Eldren, and I'm stuck here because a storm is brewing some thunder."

# TITANLORD

The soldier swallowed and pointed at the sky. "That there is no normal storm. I've been alive for quite some time, and I haven't seen anything like it yet."

Be the storm. Griffyn remembered what Ben had said when he had been frozen in time. "Could it be?" he mumbled under his breath as he scratched his lower chin.

"I beg your pardon?" the soldier said.

Griffyn tilted his head towards the soldier and winked. "You said it yourself, this storm is not normal," he then unsheathed the Masamune and started to walk towards the gate.

"I have to insist, sir, on the orders of Captain Gilkas, that you remain until the storm is settled," the soldier pleaded with him.

Griffyn looked him in the eye and lifted his sword a touch. "Do you know whose sword this is?"

The soldier nodded.

"Do you know what it can do?"

The soldier nodded again, sweat beaded on his forehead.

"Then step aside, soldier," he demanded as he walked past him.

"He's going to give me hell, you know."

Griffyn paused, if only for a moment, and turned his head a bit back. "Tell him that I intend to be the storm," he added as he kept his pace and walked through the gates.

\*\*\*

It wasn't so late that the sun was gone completely, but the rain poured heavily on the lands. Dirt had long turned to mud, and the constant sound of the raindrops touching the ground soothed Griffyn's ears. He looked towards the horizon and gazed upon the clouds that had formed.

Thunder would shake the sky apart every now and then, but through it, he only found peace. He knew that it was no coincidence, with all this talk of a storm between him and the ghost of Benjen; it had to mean something.

Griffyn took slow but heavy steps as he battled against the raging thunderstorm. His boots sunk about half an inch with every step he took. Patience was required for him to get on the road again, in hopes of reaching Kaven in time and to stop a glooming future from occurring.

As soon as he could see the main road that lead to Fort Eldren, he stopped and smiled. His hair was soaked and his clothes were drenched, but alas, he wouldn't stop. The main path was narrow and covered by tall trees and lush grass on either side.

Lightning tore from the clouds and hit the ground right in front of Griffyn. Dust rose as he covered his face from the debris.

Griffyn halted for a moment, waiting for the dust to settle. When he opened his eyes, he saw someone standing in his way. He blocked the path to the main road; the area where he needed to go desperately. He wasn't sure if he would make it in time at this point, but what he did know was that he had to get there at all costs.

He unsheathed the Masamune.

Griffyn took a deep breath as few moments went by and not one of them spoke. Their eyes met amidst the silence of the storm. "I had a feeling this weather wasn't natural, but I didn't imagine the King of the Gods himself was behind it. Is this your idea of a victory?"

"Put down your blade. I am not here to instigate conflict," Nepherin said. He didn't move, nor did he have any weapons on him. "Why do you persist in your futile resistance? You are not at all powerful that you'd be able to save the world, but you're not at all weak either that you'd just lay down and die."

Griffyn glared at him and sheathed his sword. "What gives you the right?" he asked.

"Hm?" Nepherin leaned closer.

"The prophecy you claim destined this world to die can be read from either side. It could easily mean the Titans need to stop the Gods."

"And your role in this is what exactly?"

"I'm not meant to intervene. That same prophecy that brought you here also foretold that this whole thing would happen. I saw it once, in Fort Eldren. Deep beneath the catacombs, in a secret cave hidden from the rest of the world."

Nepherin still didn't move. It was as if he was waiting

for something, or someone. It was clear he wasn't going to let him walk past anytime soon. "The Tree of Creation?"

"That's just it. Titans and Gods were branches on the tree. What do you think the tree represents?" Griffyn answered.

Nepherin sighed. "You mean to tell me that Gods and Titans were meant to be a part of life, not dictate it?"

"Whatever do you think a tree means? You were branches. Branches fall and get broken. What I'm saying is that it doesn't matter; prophecies are all full of shit regardless."

Nepherin laughed as he stepped to the left. "Come, Titanlord," he beckoned as he waved the way past him. "No harm will come to you, until you reach the Fort at least, until we meet again."

Griffyn's gaze shifted. Perhaps this was the only time he would get to size up the King of Gods. The golden spiked helmet shined even against the rain; his body covered completely with pristine white armor. He couldn't tell if it was the condition of the armor or if it was Nepherin's properties that seemed to reflect the light itself.

The only exposed areas were just below his mouth, between the bottom of his neck, and the back of his hands, which were embedded with long thick feathers of some bird.

Griffyn took slow steps. When he passed him, his hair stood on end as a strange aura grazed his presence. Goose-

# TITANLORD

bumps arose on his skin and a chill ran down his spine. It was a feeling unlike anything he had ever felt before. He held his breath and swallowed.

Time never progressed slower than in that moment. This would be his final test. This would be his final battle to rid the world of the terrible plight cast upon them.

# CHAPTER 28

## *Hold*

Natasha stood in the courtyard of Fort Eldren. She had given the command to blow the catacombs after Dwellers surged from within, threatening to overtake them. She remembered the commands that Benjen had given her, that Fort Eldren was sacred, and under no circumstances should it fall into enemy hands. Those were his parting words. But alas, she stood...her back to the pile of dust that was everything she had known for quite some time now.

"General! They're here!" one of the soldiers called to her.

Natasha took a deep breath and exhaled slowly. She balled her hands into fists, clenching tight. She gritted her teeth. Dammit, there's no hope for reinforcements, is there? She wondered, but then shook her head. The soldiers could not sense the doubt that grew like poison within her; the battle would then be over before it begun. "Man the wall, and send word that every abled soldier is to gather in the square," she demanded as she took a few steps towards the gates.

Rory, until you get back to me, I will not waver. I'll hold this fort against the Gods themselves if I need to, but please... please return to me, okay? She thought to herself.

Horns of battle sounded. Everyone rushed towards the Fort's defense, but Natasha quickly scaled up the wall and casted her gaze upon the surrounding area. Fort Eldren was built atop a steep hill, a natural defense barrier against any who would think to siege it.

Only a fool would besiege such a fort, she had heard her commander mention many times. Her eyes laid on a sea of darkness, moving ever so steadily towards them. "They're moving like a real army..." she said under her breath, scratching the back of her head. "We're not fighting against mortals, so it's safe to assume that they don't care about their lives... just what are they planning to do..."

She noticed a trail of soldiers outside the Fort. She squinted her eyes enough to make the details. "That's... our banner," she pondered for a moment as she scratched her lower chin. "Maybe it'll work."

"General," one of the soldiers interrupted her thoughts as he stepped beside her. She glanced at him and sighed.

"Speak."

"The men are worried... The commander isn't here,

and-"

She turned her head to the courtyard from her position on the wall. Everyone paused to look up at their beloved general.

"We swore an oath when we took arms back in Palleria. Do you still remember it?" she asked, and there was silence. "Look!" she said as she pointed over the wall behind her. "Beyond lays a terrible darkness that comes not only for us, but for every man, woman, and child that walk this world..." she sighed. "If you fight today, you will most likely die here."

The silence thickened and tension rose. Natasha's brows narrowed and her face reddened. "I ask you, brothers and sisters, is this not the darkness we swore to fend off?" she questioned before taking out her dual swords that rested on her back.

"Every life is beautiful because it has an ending, and in this, I am no different than you. We all may die today. With luck, we might die tomorrow; in the end, it's all meaningless," she paused to take a deep breath. "Every time we face such moments, we repeat the words 'of the light, by the light' and that means something, dammit!"

She stopped for a moment and scanned the faces of the soldiers that looked up to her. They were tense, some were shaking. The veterans had all left with The Red Hand, and with him, went most of the generals. Natasha was the Second, and that still carried some weight, but the soldiers here weren't the veterans that won the major battles that they've been in; of that she was aware.

"I have faced these things before, and I was victorious. We cannot afford to treat this as any normal attack. So, I ask you to have confidence and trust that each one of us here is worth ten of them in open battle," she encouraged with a wavering voice. She turned her head towards the gatekeepers and nodded at them. "Open the gates," she demanded.

The silence broke. A buzzing sound began to rise once she gave the command. The gatekeeper's jaws nearly touch the ground, gasping at what lay beyond.

"We stand a better chance if we take them on directly and treat them like the mindless animals that they are. Archers will remain on the walls and back us up. This, I swear to you, is our best chance to survive," she said as she scaled down the wall and stood tall in front of her soldiers.

"I beg of you," she pleaded as her voice cracked. "Die, right here, with me!"

# CHAPTER 29

## *Rise, Titanlord*

**G**riffyn moved as fast as his legs allowed him. He had wasted so much time already; he had stopped and rested when he needed, but his best option right now was to catch up to Kaven before they engaged the siege. It was a race against time to stop whatever fate he had seen in the Citadel. *I'm coming, Kaven, Natasha, just hold on,* he thought to himself.

The path disappeared. Griffyn paused for a moment as he quickly scanned his surroundings. The tall trees intertwined with one another, almost as if they purposely intended to hide the fort. Perhaps this was nature's way of preserving the past.

*Come on, think!* he said to himself. He scratched the back of his head, then spotted something on a tree trunk to his right. "What's this?" Griffyn wondered before he stepped closer to inspect it. He placed his hand on the bark and moved it across the engraving. A cross. "Thanks," he smiled.

He lifted his head and could see a few more trees that were engraved. He didn't know who had made them, but at this point, it was his best option.

He followed the engravings. By traveling alone, he would be able to reach the fort faster, but a problem remained: Fort Eldren was made so that it wouldn't be found. He was once there, but he had been blindfolded when Tatiana Hunter had saved him and Rory after they got captured by bandits.

This time, it would be his turn to return the favor, but somehow, he had to reach it before the end began. Nepherin himself had visited him. He didn't understand why. Was it possible that the King of the Gods himself was beginning to doubt this crusade of his?

He was running. He didn't say a single word, but his mind was buzzing with dwindled thoughts of the siege. Last he remembered, Natasha had sent him and Rory away from the Fort to deal with the army. He felt confident that Natasha would win, but in all that time, Natasha was fighting an unwinnable fight. She was still fighting. Her commander died to save him. What becomes of a daunted heart that begs to be forgiven?

Griffyn had to atone, and the only way he could do that was to stop this blight from ever happening. He alone was the key, but there was something else he was wrestling with. Veda had warned Rory not to look back; every word uttered by the Titans or Gods seemed to have some form of absolution. Until we meet again. Nepherin's words echoed in his mind like a looming dagger hanging over Griffyn's head.

The mountains behind him seemed to grow taller and taller with every pace he covered. He was getting closer now, much closer. The rain had stopped, but the terrain was still muddy, and the lush grasses carried much of the dust that had settled in after the army had marched by. He was on the right track, of that he was certain.

He noticed a steep hill that came into view just past some trees. That would be a good place to get a better view before proceeding further, he thought. He dashed against the winds and trees until a sound echoed in his ears.

The smell of burnt ashes reached him as he gazed upon Fort Eldren. A lonely building that rested on a slope surrounded by mountains, the Wide Sea guarding its rear. Yet even then, he squinted his eyes to make out the details of what was going on. The front walls -flanked by two guard towers- were bombarding the demons below. The gate remained shut -thankfully, but there was something else he noticed as well.

A group of soldiers were engaging the right side of the assault, while the left side began piling on top of each other, forming some form of tower to breach the wall.

What will you do, Titanlord?

# TITANLORD

He heard the voice again. "I thought it was your job to provide the answers," Griffyn spat as his lips formed into a thin line. He tilted his head left. "That must be Kaven, engaging them after the demons mobilized. Natasha was smart, she blew up the Keep to stop the horde from pouring in the other side. Both Natasha and Kaven have made all the right choices, leading me to right here and right now. Thus, there is but one option."

Griffyn took out the Masamune and swept it to his left, swinging it as fast as he could. The blast that came out traveled across the land and grew bigger the more distance it covered.

The blast did its purpose. It plastered the demons on the left against the fortified wall, crushing many of them with such force that he thought some form of paste was running down the walls.

The cries of the soldiers cheering could be heard across the distance between Griffyn and them. He then looked down towards the ground. He stood atop the hill; it seemed deep, but the slope downwards wasn't too sharp. "Will I make it?"

You have the Strength. You will.

Griffyn smirked, and then glanced up for a minute. "Here goes nothing," he muttered as he began to run down the hill with all his might. "If I start running and speed up proportionately, I should be able to make this," he said as he increased his speed the further down he got. If he was like any other mortal, this would've been a mistake, but for some reason, Griffyn's legs seemed to cope well.

His strike decimated half the assault, but he knew he couldn't swing at the walls again. The damage that it caused to the demons had also harmed the stone. He didn't know if another blast would bring the walls down or not.

"I'm coming everyone, please... just hold on for a little while longer," he prayed under his breath as he reached the bottom of the hill. A flat plain and a few inches of running up a hill was all that was between him and the Fort. The demons had sensed his presence after the blast. They changed the direction of their assault and charged straight towards Griffyn.

The louder the growls got, the louder a ferocious growl erupted from his chest. He was ready, sword in hand. A few of them jumped at Griffyn as they neared, but he quickly dodged to the left and swung upwards, with the blast throwing them further into the air. Griffyn kept running.

Another slash to the right, and then to the left. He kept running to reach the top as fast as he could. A sigh of relief escaped his lips as he reached the front lines of battle. There were a few good seconds of silence as he took in the surroundings. Every soldier and demon alike knew that the cavalry had arrived. A symbol, who stood on equal grounds with all the brave heroes of old, had reached the final setting stage, the fate of the world hanging on the balance.

Griffyn took a quick glance at the situation. His blast earlier had stopped the demons from almost reaching the top of the wall, but it did not destroy all of them. He was isolated at the back, severely outnumbered by the demons on his left.

The silence ended then. The demons rallied, and a good portion of them charged towards Griffyn. "Shit, I can't just blast again. I'll hit Kaven..." he realized as he readied his stance.

Shortly after, the gates of the Fort opened.

"Charge!" Natasha's voice echoed from behind a swell of soldiers that rushed out the gates, striking the demons from the back.

"Now!" Griffyn yelled as he began to run towards the Dwellers. Their right was engaged, and now their left was about to collapse.

Pause.

He heard the voice say as he used his power to stop. "Why?" he asked. "Now is the best time to render this effective. We only have one chance."

There's no point in reaching the battle only to rush towards your death. You can't use Pollus here. You will be swallowed in that sea of darkness.

Griffyn gritted his teeth and swore. "Then what can be done?" he asked.

Nothing. This battle is already won.

"Yeah, this battle," he said with a sighed.

"Look out!" He heard Natasha shout. He turned his head left and dashed to the side, swinging at the Dweller that appeared.

Behind you.

Griffyn lowered his body as he swung to his right, then followed it up with another right swing. Dwellers were falling off, as bees would drive a threat from its hive.

"Griffyn!" Natasha shouted at him. Worry filled her voice. This was the first time she was seeing him since she sent both him and Rory to the Capital to meet Ben. So many stories and so many sleepless nights fighting, never allowed her a moment of peace.

"Hold, Natasha! Push onwards!" Griffyn shouted back. He couldn't see how Kaven was fairing, but he was willing to bet that he was doing just fine. A few rouge Dwellers charged at him but proved little resistance. He rolled behind them and swung the sword, blasting them down the hill.

Then a screech ripped through the surrounding skies. The Dwellers calmed down as heavy footsteps began to rustle in everyone's ears. The Dwellers retreated for only a moment, and then tilted their heads towards the horizon as they squealed.

"What's going on?" Griffyn asked as he squinted his gaze to make out the details of someone walking towards them. He was dressed in full plated armor. Dawn was coming, and the rays of the sun reflected in its armor. It

# TITANLORD

shone brilliantly, but Griffyn felt his insides turn.

"Come now, mortals. You have all brought this upon yourselves." It was the Dwellers lord. "Step forth, son of man. Let the rains of a thousand ashes descend upon you!"

Griffyn stood still. A chill ran down his spine, his grip tightening on the Masamune and sweat beaded down his forehead. This would be his final test.

# CHAPTER 30

## *Pride*

Griffyn analyzed the battle before him; the Dweller ranks had taken heavy losses, but were winning the battle so far. However, now that they were all distracted by their lord's emergence, he looked at Natasha and pointed with his brows.

"Get back inside!" Natasha shouted, and the soldiers all sounded a cry as they ran towards the gate.

Griffyn sprinted as fast as he could. He had to take a better position and force the Dweller Lord to do battle on Griffyn's own terms. Though breaking formation in the midst of a battle had dire consequences, he knew that if they acted fast, then they could achieve it just in time.

As Kaven's forces also began their retreat inside,

# TITANLORD

Griffyn saw the Dweller Lord raise his hand. All Dwellers in the vicinity halted.

Griffyn passed by the gate. "Shut the gates!" he bellowed as he slid inside, his chest heaving. He felt a hand on his shoulder and turned his head to see Natasha and Kaven. A smile broke out on his lips that stretched from ear to ear, as he hugged the former, he closed his eyes and took a deep breath. "I'm sorry," he mumbled.

"We'll talk later, okay?" Natasha comforted as her gaze fixated on the gate. She had missed Griffyn and had much to discuss, but she knew that this wasn't the end of the horde outside. "What's next?"

Griffyn pulled away from her embrace and scanned his surroundings. The courtyard was filled with broken swords and shields. The smell of iron wafted into the air. It was as if they had been sieged for years. "What happened here?" he asked when he saw the Keep. He couldn't make the top from the bottom; Its once tall walls were now crumbled pieces of rubble. The stones tore to pieces by a seemingly unimaginable force.

"Our best idea to shut down the other horde."

"The other horde?" Kaven chimed in.

"They came from the catacombs," Natasha replied.

"Wait, do you hear that?"

It was subtle, but someone was walking steadily towards them. He paused as he got closer. A thud sounded as the gates of Fort Eldren burst off their hinges. A gust of rubble rose from the ground as the gate slammed into the ground. "Fall back!" Natasha shouted.

The soldiers hurried away, but there was nowhere to go. "Fall back to where, Nat?" Kaven cried as he unsheathed his sword. "Soldiers! On me!" he shouted at the top of his lungs.

"Wait," Griffyn said as he stared into the pile of dust. He could make the details of that being, anywhere and at any time. "He's here," he warned as he took a few steps forward.

"Remember what I told you when we first met?" The Dweller Lord drawled as he kept his eyes fixed on Griffyn's. He took off his helmet and a large grin overtook him, showing those white fangs as his left eye twitched. "Do as you may, but you are mortal. And all mortals tremble before us."

Griffyn placed his hand on the Masamune's hilt. A rattling noise rose. "Kaven, Natasha, scale up the walls and be on the lookout for any tricks," Griffyn broke his silence. His heartbeat was steady, but only because he was breathing in slow and exhaling even slower.

"You can't be serious..." Natasha huffed.

"Listen to me," Griffyn shot back at her without shifting his gaze or moving a muscle.

Kaven placed a hand on her shoulder. "He's not the same kid you knew when you sent them off," he said, then turned around and climbed up the walls.

Natasha took slow steps following Kaven but then turned her face towards Griffyn. "Be safe..." she said as she looked the other way and continued after Kaven.

Griffyn smiled as he unsheathed his sword and cracked his neck. "There is no point in dwelling any further. Let's settle this, right here and right now."

The Dweller Lord smirked at him. "This is bemusing. I cannot fathom a mortal that dares defy the Gods, but here you are, and here you stand. I will pay you the respect of putting you down quickly at least."

"Tell me, demon. What makes you believe that you can strike not one but two Titans?"

The Dweller Lord pulled his head back. "Oh? It's Titans against Gods now, is it?"

Griffyn shook his head. "It's a Titanlord against a glorified demon filth," he said as he took a few steps towards him. The Dweller Lord's expression changed, as he picked up his weapon, the Golden Warhammer. It was at least twice as tall as Griffyn, with a sharped finish towards the other end.

The Dweller Lord swung his hammer from above. Griffyn swung from the opposite side, and the two clashed. The collision sent shockwaves through the courtyard. The Warhammer did more damage than Griffyn had expected. He parried and lost his footing.

Roll to the right.

The Dweller Lord followed up with another swing,

but Griffyn dodged it. "It'll take more than just strength and counsel to win a battle, mortal. Allow me to demonstrate the difference between knowing how to win, and actually winning a battle," he said before swinging at him again.

Roll again, then get up and instantly step back.

Griffyn did as Veda advised, but there was something about this fight that didn't seem right. For the first time since he held the Masamune, he was on the defensive.

"What's wrong, little boy? Or Titanlord, is it?" the Dweller Lord shouted as he kept hammering hits at him. Griffyn was barely able to dodge them, his chest heaved with the effort it extorted.

Control your breathing.

"Shut up!" Griffyn shouted. "Shut up! Leave me to this! Enough of you!"

There was silence for but a moment as the Dweller Lord paused. "Lost your mind, boy?"

Griffyn shouted at the top of his lungs. Veda remained silent this time. He tightened his grip on the sword and lunged towards the Dweller Lord. The Masamune collided with the Warhammer one more, only this time, the shockwave didn't push Griffyn back. He held on and put more weight into his strike. His vision began to grow hazy for a moment.

"Your... eyes... they changed colors," the Dweller Lord gasped before he took a step back and looked hard at

Griffyn's pupils. An orange hue enveloped his iris's. "Pollus..." he whispered under his breath.

Griffyn swung the sword towards the Dweller again. The wave pushed everything past him back into the wall, save for the Dweller Lord who struggled to keep his footing.

"You... swine," the Dweller Lord mumbled as he straightened his arms, bringing the Warhammer ahead of his body. The weight of his weapon eased his positioning.

But Griffyn appeared, almost out of thin air, right in front of him. He swung the Masamune against him. The Dweller Lord's eyes widened as he shoved the Warhammer in front of the Masamune. The two weapons collided again, only this time, the Warhammer shattered.

The Dweller Lord's face twitched, and his jaw almost touched the ground. His eyes... are so fierce, he thought to himself. As Griffyn was focused on his momentum, the Dweller Lord grabbed the dagger at his waist and shoved it into his chest.

Griffyn was halted in his run. The breath in his chest escaped through his lips, and he coughed as he choked on something thick. Blood spurt out suddenly, his eyes widened too, as he felt the taste of cold hard steel into his guts. He staggered back slowly. The world danced around him though he stood still.

"Griffyn!" Natasha screamed at the top of her lungs. Her shout echoed through the air and filled the entire courtyard.

"You scared me for a second," the Dweller Lord muttered before taking a few steps closer. "If you were to join us, I have no doubt that you would have a superior rank. Shame that you chose to oppose what you do not understand," he added as he took a few more steps towards to Griffyn.

Griffyn was still standing, though, his vision blurred. "I'm sorry, Ven," he muttered as his grip lightened on the sword, and he fell forward.

The Dweller Lord caught him. He lifted him up a bit and swung his knife at his chest again. Blood poured out of the large gash. "Your power was worthy enough to merit my appearance. At least take pride in that, Titanlord."

# CHAPTER 31

## *The King Without a Crown*

**N**atasha was screaming and began running back towards the battlefield. But no amount of speed would be enough.

"Natasha!" Kaven shouted, his heart was beating inside his chest too. They had witnessed it, far away from the safety of the walls... the moment the dagger had slid into Griffyn's chest. He gritted his teeth so hard that blood almost came out.

"Amusing, wouldn't you say?" Kaven heard a voice behind him.

He swallowed and turned around slowly. "Nepherin..." he muttered as he gazed upon the King of the Gods, who was suddenly resting on top of the wall. How long was he here?

"His name is Dilmur. The Bringer of Pain," Nepherin added.

Kaven tried to speak, or even just move an inch of muscle, but couldn't. Someone even more powerful than the Dweller Lord was beside him. Right there.

"I understand why someone so simple would be hypnotized by his charisma. Of that, I offer you no resentment. Be it a testament to his ability and his legacy. The time of the Titans has now ended. There is none capable of wielding that sword."

"W... why..." Kaven finally broke his silence. "Why do you insist on killing us all..."

"For the same reason you insist on living," Nepherin got down from his post and began making his way towards the stairs that lead down to the courtyard. Natasha was on her way to face off against Dilmur. "But honestly, there is no reason, there is no prophecy. Our father has abandoned us. It is not yet clear to my brothers, but I am certain of it. This world is now ours. Ours to destroy, or ours to save."

He walked to the edge of the stairs. His face twitched as his left brow shot up. "Kneel," he commanded, his voice echoing far across the Fort. Kaven, his soldiers, and even Natasha, who was at the courtyard, now felt compelled to obey him. This wasn't a trick, nor some sort of power that Nepherin had. They felt obliged to do as he commanded, as though they had no other choice.

He smiled as they fell to their knees, yet Nepherin's

eyes widened suddenly, his hair standing on end as he looked out into the courtyard. A gentle white light glowed from where Griffyn's body laid. "Unbelievable..." Nepherin muttered, a gasp escaping him.

Dilmur stumbled back from the corpse as a gentle swaying light began to emit from Griffyn's body. "It can't be..." Dilmur muttered as his breath became short. A man then appeared next to Griffyn. "What do you think you're doing?"

Dilmur rushed towards the man with his knife, but stopped when the man lifted a hand and pointed at him. Dilmur froze.

"Don't you dare touch him!" Natasha screamed at the man as she tried to get up. For some reason, she found that she couldn't stand. He was on one knee too and had his right hand atop Griffyn's head. He was moving his lips. There was a still silence that beckoned the heart of everyone in the courtyard.

The man's lips stopped, and he stood. He took a quick glance at his surroundings. All but Dilmur, the Dwellers, and Nepherin were on their knees. He shifted his gaze towards Natasha. "I am the Light," he said to her.

Those words cut through Natasha's heart as a warm knife cut through butter. She felt at ease. The overwhelming heart ache of Griffyn's death dissipated from her chest. The tears on her face were nothing but warm water easing her soul.

"Behold. The man without a crown, a broken coward

who hid far back inside his castle all for a shadow... What now, man? What becomes of your world, your fiefs and all those Kings rule over when there are no kings left?" Nepherin wondered, walking down the steps as he smirked at the man.

The man's eyes met with Nepherin's. "I may be without a crown, but I am still a king," he said before he took a breath. "Rise," he commanded, and everyone was free to move again.

Nepherin grinned. "Stop him, stop him now, Dilmur!"

Dilmur could suddenly move again. He lunged at the man and pushed his hand forward enough so that the knife would enter his neck. But, as he moved closer towards him, another figure appeared beside the stranger and swung a sword towards him. A familiar sword.

The sword slashed Dilmur clean across the chest. He fell on his back growling and wreathing in the sand until he ceased moving, the last breath escaping him.

"You claim superiority when you have none. Any who follow the path of destruction must be prepared to bathe in its wake. Do you see the light now, Dilmur?" A familiar voice said.

"Griffyn..." Natasha said as she approached him, tears running down her cheeks again.

"Nepherin... where is he?" Griffyn mumbled through blood-soaked lips, his eyes glowing purple.

The man turned towards him. "He's long gone."

# TITANLORD

Griffyn's eyes met with the stranger. For the first time since he set foot outside the village, Griffyn's stress eased at his presence. He waved his hand against his chest, the wounds closing of their own accord.

"The scars remain, I'm afraid."

Griffyn lifted his head and looked at the Dweller Lord. His body began to deteriorate. He then shifted his gaze upon all the Dwellers that had entered the Fort and were rooting for their Lord. They all were screeching, as if they could feel the pain of their lord.

"Peril to thy, my God... I submit to you my will and my life. I offer you my soul, so that you may devour it... Woe unto the Pretender, and upon those who oppose you..." Dilmur spouted with the last of his breath as his body broke down and reduced to ashes.

A gentle breeze played against Griffyn's skin as he turned his face towards the Dwellers. They soon joined their Lord, each leaving behind nothing but a pile of ashes. He tilted his head and glanced at Natasha. She stood there, silent. Tears still streaming down her cheeks.

"Griffyn?" she muttered in disbelief.

Griffyn took a deep breath and smiled. Natasha rushed towards him, falling to her knees for an embrace. She held on to him and squeezed. Griffyn gently pushed her away and groaned as he sat up. "Natasha..."

"I'm sorry," she mumbled as she gently touched his chest. His skin was still pink where the dagger had cut him. "The scar... it's still there," she said to him. "But I saw you..." she added before she leaned back on her heels. "I saw him..."

The man stepped towards Natasha. "I don't have a lot of time to explain everything, but it is rather important that I speak to him. Alone."

Natasha staggered to her feet. She had so many questions, but she knew now was not the right time for them. Kaven stood next to her, running to the courtyard the moment the stranger appeared, and grabbed her. "Come on, we have a lot of things to catch up on together," he said as he began to walk away. "I'm glad you didn't die, kiddo," he muttered to Griffyn as he kept walking.

Griffyn looked after them and sighed, climbing to his feet. "I did... die. But I returned," he said as he rolled his hands into fists and then spread them open a couple times. The sword fell. He turned his hands around and kept his gaze fixed on them. He glanced up at the man. "Can you do it again? Can you bring others back? Is that your power?" he asked, a moment of hope flashing into his mind.

The man shook his head. "None may alter creation or the natural order of life and death. Except when something grand transpires. You weren't meant to die here today, Griffyn. You were meant to travel somewhere else."

"What?" Griffyn squinted and narrowed his brows. "Who are you? Nepherin knew you... he was afraid of you."

# TITANLORD

The man sighed. "I have had many names. More than I can remember, but my real name is Robert R. Magmar, The First."

"You're a Magmar, The First? How is that possible?"

"How is it possible that you possess Titan Powers? Don't ask pointless questions."

"How about this then, where were you?" Griffyn asked as veins beaded on his forehead. "Where were you when your sons and daughters ravished the lands? Where were you when a Magmar got a little girl expelled from her village and was killed in his castle? Your castle?"

"It's better to show you, I think."

Griffyn took a step back.

Robert sighed. "Volos trakidoias"

He is Colossal. A Titan as well. Better known as Robrin, the Red Knight.

"So, now you show up too?" Griffyn said at Veda's voice.

"He had no choice. You commanded as such, or have you forgotten?" Robrin said as he looked him in the eye. "I'm not judging you; Veda of all people knows that I am not without sins, but those of this Magmar? You cannot pin on me. He was no true Magmar."

"What are you saying?" Griffyn asked.

"I took an oath never to engage in the politics of the world again, but now I've broken that oath, for you. The scales were not in balance, and that is why I broke my slumber."

Griffyn narrowed his brows as sweat beaded on his forehead.

"This is a lot to take, I know, but now that I've interfered, there is but a moment in which you can strike."

"You were there... in the Citadel, weren't you? It was you who broke Nepherin's connection to the Divine."

Robrin nodded. "This was a last measure, in order to level the playing field."

Griffyn shook his head. "You speak of war as if it's a game. But how many faces will I never see again? Why did you save me and not Ben?"

"You are Filius," Robrin said as he took a step closer towards him. He placed a hand on his shoulder. "You have been brave; you have taken everything on your shoulders. No one knows the weight of each step that you take, but ask yourself this, if that weight came upon another, would they be able to bear it?"

"But is it just? That I be raised from the dead when so many have fallen before me?" Griffyn lowered his head. "It's too heavy..."

"Justice?" Robrin leaned his head back. "You walk the path of justice. But to arrive at its summit, there's something you still lack."

"And what is that?"

"You will learn it, sooner rather than later."

# TITANLORD

Griffyn lifted his head and looked Robrin in the eye. "I don't pertain to the laws of men, nor monarchs or kings or emperors. I only do what I think is right."

"And that remains your weakness."

"In what manner? Are you saying that I need to follow a monarch or a deity's formation of justice?"

Robrin shook his head. "Justice is justice, Griffyn. It knows no allies, nor enemies... you included."

Griffyn shook his head. "There's so much left to learn."

Robrin placed a hand on his shoulder. "Don't dwell. Just concentrate and become who you can be, make any decision you must... so that you aren't swallowed next time."

Griffyn tilted his head a bit and sighed. "I have looked their King in the eye. He cannot devour me."

"Then quell your Titans, lest they quell you," Robrin advised as he slowly moved his hand away from Griffyn. The words hit him harder than he expected.

Griffyn looked around, everything had returned to normal. Natasha rushed towards him, Kaven at her heels. "Griffyn!" she shouted as she stood next to him. "Who is he?" she asked looking at the strange man.

"He's a king," Griffyn said with a smile.

"What?" Natasha and Kaven gasped.

"Where will you go?" Griffyn asked. Robrin had

turned his back and began to walk away.

Robrin paused and turned around to face them. "I must return to slumber. I have jeopardized the grand plan enough already," he said as he smiled and waved at Griffyn. As he began walking again, Griffyn couldn't help but feel the burden on his shoulders lift a bit. He looked around him, and saw Natasha, with tears running down her cheeks, and Kaven standing tall next to her.

Every soldier at the Fort had stopped and stepped closer towards him. Griffyn was completely encircled by them. Kaven took the first step forward and paused before him.

Kaven staggered a bit, but then kneeled.

Natasha rushed towards him and forced him up. "That is not your decision to make. Whoever you intend to bend your knee to, you will not break your oath to Ben, nor to me, do you understand, moron?" Natasha growled at him.

Kaven narrowed his brows. "Can you see nothing, Natasha?" he paused and began to take heavy breaths. "This is what Ben spoke of. This is the plan. He is the plan!" he cried as he pointed towards Griffyn.

The soldiers began to debate amongst themselves, their discussion echoing far and wide across the Fort.

Griffyn lifted his hand and instilled silence. He sighed. "I ask none to bend their knee, nor have I asked of anyone to follow me," he admitted as he took a deep breath. "Stop

# TITANLORD

bickering amongst yourselves while the shadows grow stronger!" he shouted. He took a few breaths. "You, men of the Light, are what stands between us and true darkness from overtaking everything and everyone you have ever known and loved." He curled his hands into fists. "Does it truly matter who rules over you when there is no kingdom but turned to ash?"

"We are not bickering amongst ourselves," Natasha said as she stepped forward. "I, the Second, was given the task that, should the commander perish, I was to nominate a contender. A protector who can deliver us from darkness-"

"I care not about who emerges as a protector, but I say this to you, the Gods have conspired to bring ruin to us all," Griffyn said, as his tone broke. "Let us be the difference. Let all of us swear allegiance right now, not to a man, titan, nor god, but to truth, justice and light," his voice faded. As he picked up the Masamune from the ground. "Let us prove to everyone that good still exists, and that we value our dead."

The soldiers roared as they began to chant his title. "Titanlord! Titanlord! Titanlord!"

Griffyn smiled.

Natasha paced back and forth as she thought about his words, until Kaven grabbed hold of her. "Is there anything really left to think about?" he said to her, and she tilted her head.

Natasha freed herself from Kaven and walked towards Griffyn. She unsheathed her sword and bowed in front of him. "It is as you said. Let us swear allegiance not to anything else but the good in us."

# CHAPTER 32

## *Vengeance*

riffyn stood in the midst of the courtyard. He grabbed his chest and gently moved his hand over where the knife struck him. His pupils dilated, and he squinted his eyes.

"Griffyn," Natasha said as she placed a hand on his shoulder. "Does it still hurt?" she asked.

Griffyn's eyes laid open. He looked at her and smiled. "It's as if it didn't happen," he said as he took a few steps towards gate. "How's the repairs going?"

"It'll take a while, but it'll get there."

Griffyn's eyes pulsed and sparked blue.

There is something brewing in the darkness.

"When is it not," Griffyn sighed out loud.

"Pardon?" Natasha asked. Griffyn nodded his head and took a few steps ahead.

"What darkness?"

Nepherin was a child of atrocious behavior. He would never show up here if there was a shred of a chance of your victory. No, their powers far surpass ours in this matter. I must believe that it was dictated that you would fall on this day.

"The Grand Plan..." Griffyn pondered, ignoring the looks from Natasha.

Yes. Colossal changed things no doubt, but that leaves a possibility of survival, God or not.

"What are you saying? It's not like you haven't been wrong before."

That's just it. When I spoke to you, telling you to go south, it was to stop something.

"Stop what?"

Three horns suddenly erupted through the air. The sound tore at their surroundings, replacing the tension with panic in their hearts. Soldiers spread out, and Griffyn placed his hand on the hilt of his sword.

"What's this?" he asked.

"It's ours..." Natasha said as she took a few steps closer.

Can we win another war so soon? Griffyn pondered the thought. He glanced at the ground beneath him and swore. He took a deep breath, and then scanned his surroundings.

"They're exhausted," he said.

"They will do as commanded. Of that, I assure you."

"It's not mutiny that worries me," Griffyn said as he tilted his head towards the gate keepers. "Open the gates."

"Griffyn!" Natasha said as she rushed towards him. "You can't-"

Griffyn's eyes met with hers. They were hollow, fearless. Shivers shot down her spine at their intensity. She tried to speak but couldn't.

Natasha nodded at the soldiers guarding the gates, and they obeyed. The gates shrieked as they opened slowly, riling up the rubble and dust that had gathered next to it.

Two men appeared in front of the gate, behind them laid an army of at least three thousand. One of the men that stepped forward wore armor that resembled Kaven's.

"You?" Griffyn mumbled as his brows narrowed. He tightened his grip on the Masamune. "You were there, with Dale, weren't you?" he asked.

"The name's Edgar," he said as he nodded at Griffyn. "Hello, Nat," he greeted as he shifted his head towards her.

Natasha grimaced at him but remained silent.

Griffyn leaned to the side, looking at the men accompanying him. "Teetans? South of Wynne. You were the one who intercepted our men in their attempt to make contact?"

Edgar nodded. "I noticed the party that you sent out, I thought it... useful to follow them."

Griffyn's eyes dilated. "Why are you here?"

Edgar glanced at the ground. "It wasn't difficult to convince them to fight for us. The small numbers that we were, they believed in us," he explained as he looked at the Teetans behind him. "I took them to Ospis and arrived just in time to lift its siege by those Dwellers."

Griffyn pondered for a moment and sighed. "I don't know what you think you can achieve in this moment, nor why are you telling me this."

Edgar shook his head gently and stepped closer to Griffyn. As he did Natasha pulled out her twin swords. "Not so close, old friend."

Griffyn signaled her with a wave of his hand.

Edgar took a breath. "When we did take the city, as we headed inside, there was a creature there. Something the Commander called Nepherin..."

"You saw one of them?" Griffyn asked.

Edgar's brows narrowed. "One of them?"

Griffyn grinned and scratched his forehead. "What did he look like?"

Edgar staggered. "Golden helmet, two wings and could levitate. But then, suddenly something happened...

he glowed for a moment, then fell to the ground."

"His weapon, what was he holding?"

Edgar took a step back and grimaced. "This isn't news to you?"

Griffyn sighed. "They're called the New Children. Another branch from the Divine. Just like the Titans."

Edgar paused for a moment, with his jaw open. "I'm sorry. I don't mean to lose my composure, but the Commander never really shared these things with us..."

"He was protecting you from it," Griffyn said as he took a few steps towards him. "Which tells me two things, either he didn't trust what you would do with the information, or that he didn't think you ready for the fight."

"Fight them?"

Griffyn stepped away, but then turned his head to look at him from the corner of his eyes. "Gods."

Edgar unsheathed his sword at the word.

Natasha tightened her grip on her dual swords, but Griffyn put his hand on her arm and shook his head.

Edgar then took a few steps forward. His sword seemed to rattle in his hand before he dropped it. "Then tell me, Titanlord, how exactly can humanity prevail?"

Griffyn turned and faced him. "What weapon did he have?" he asked again.

"Why is that important?"

"What weapon did have?" he repeated yet again, his tone fierce.

"A bow..."

"Eros... That was the one who shot Roriana in the eye," Griffyn said. Natasha gasped and held her face, trying to stop the tears from running down her cheeks.

Griffyn took another step towards him. "When Benjen bought enough time for me and my friend to escape, I heard their King give the command. Eros was the one that ended your Commander."

"Why are you telling me this?" Edgar spoke, his tone breaking as he collapsed to his knees.

"Because up until now, none save for the Gods called me Titanlord, not because I chose it, but because they are afraid," he explained as he stood before him. "I don't doubt that you are a good man, but tell me, why did you truly come here?"

Edgar took a deep breath. "He gave us a choice... your life, for everyone else's..."

"And you believed him?"

"I did, before I saw that other... God run away from here. I thought it impossible to stand up to them, but now I see that the Commander was right in trusting you with the sword. You are the only one who can do it... you can save us!"

"I don't save cowards," Griffyn said before he swung

the Masamune. The sword hit his neck and met little resistance as it cut through his skin. Blood splattered on Griffyn's chest.

# CHAPTER 33

## *Fate of The Damned*

Natasha gawked. He felt the anxiety of the soldiers rise as their gazes fixed on him. Even with all that had happened, he had just executed someone they had all fought with.

Griffyn took a good look at them, and then dropped his sword to the ground. "Any of you who desire to fight me for what I just did, step forth and pick it up."

A soldier at the back shook his head and took a few steps towards him. He was panting, as if he had just run a marathon. "I have but one question..."

Griffyn squeezed his forehead with his hand, then tilted his head towards him. "Speak," he commanded.

"Did the voices within the sword command you to do so?"

# TITANLORD

Griffyn was taken aback by his question. "Is that what you believe? That the sword... compels me?"

"If we're to follow you to the end of the world, I think we all deserve the answer!"

Natasha lowered her head and stepped towards Griffyn. She punched him square in the face and spat on the ground at his feet.

"Natasha..." Griffyn groaned.

"Shut up," she said and turned towards the soldier. "Don't you disrespect those who have died to get us here ever again. Lest you wish to join their ranks."

Griffyn's brows narrowed, but his attention quickly averted away. Footsteps neared him.

The man accompanying Edgar took a few steps forward. He raised his hands. "I don't want to fight."

Natasha tensed and took a breath.

Griffyn looked him in the eye and signaled him to approach. "You're either very brave, or very stupid, to approach me right after I beheaded your leader."

The man smirked. "He was a cunt, and he was no leader of mine. My name's Kogart Ellis, but everyone calls me Kog. I used to lead the Militia at Ospis, until he showed up at the head of an army."

Griffyn glanced at Natasha. "Do you know who he is?"

Natasha wiped her tears and nodded. "He's one of the

Colored Knights, the Mad Dog's brother."

"Aizeya?" Griffyn asked.

Kog nodded. "I'm not too proud of my baby brother. He is said to have a... very foul tongue, but what this man said was true. If that thing that showed up was indeed a God, then dammit, I want to fight the fuckers."

The ground shook beneath their feet. "An earthquake? Now?" a soldier shouted. "A storm perhaps?" another chimed in.

Griffyn scratched his head. He looked at Kog. "Stay here," he commanded as he picked up the Masamune and turned his gaze towards the rubble blocking the main keep.

He swung the Masamune, and a gust of wind flew across to the stones, clearing the way. Natasha tried to follow, but he raised his hand. "I'll call for you if I need you."

Griffyn walked through the narrow corridors, sword in hand, slipping through the rubble inside. There was something glowing at the end. His heartbeat rose, and he could feel his pulse through his skin.

With every step he took, his blood heated even more, almost boiling him from within. The pressure was unlike anything he had ever experienced. He stopped in front of a door, with not a scratch on it. Nothing. As if time had frozen for that part of the entire keep. The glow was coming from inside.

He took a breath and gently opened the door. Nepherin

stood at the far end of the room, gazing through the window at the horizon. Griffyn's heart almost jumped out of his chest. He froze where he stood.

"I used the last of my powers to restore this room," Nepherin said. "This used to be the seat of power. In this room, in all of history, the occupant had the weight of the world on his shoulders."

Griffyn couldn't stop looking at Nepherin. Why was he here, of all the places? Hadn't he run the moment Colossal showed himself, when he brought Griffyn back from the dead.

"Do you understand what I'm telling you?" Nepherin asked.

Griffyn remained silent.

Nepherin shook his head. "You came back!" It was the first time Griffyn had ever heard Nepherin's voice rise, even in the slightest.

"So?" he broke his silence.

"Have you learned nothing? Colossal himself gives his life away so that you may live, and you still do not see..."

"Colossal is just a Titan..."

Nepherin shook his head. "He was the First Titan."

"I thought that was Veda," Griffyn wondered.

"Veda was their king, but not their first."

Griffyn's brows narrowed. "So, is that it? You misread

a prophecy? You misunderstood your father's message?"

"You speak as if you're mortal, just like the rest of them. But tell me, what did you see when you perished? When your soul was torn from your body? Of what can you speak?"

Griffyn lowered his head. "Nothing. Nepherin, there was nothing but emptiness. A great void…"

Nepherin staggered, then stood still. He took short breaths and finally turned around to face him. "You think the world so simple, because I am the edge of your world, Titanlord," he said, panting.

"Right now, you're the only one threatening it."

Nepherin grinned. The light of the sun rising from the east radiated against his broken gold helmet. He spread his arms wide. "Then go ahead. Strike me down and gaze beyond me."

Griffyn fixed his eyes unto him. He gritted his teeth as his brows narrowed again. He took careful and slow steps towards him.

The closer he got to Nepherin, the more he felt a shiver run down his spine. All the hair on his body stood still. He tightened his grip on the Masamune and lifted it high.

"In the name of the Red Hand, Roriana, Vendel and all those who perished by your hand or your doings…" Before he could swing, something startled him and he paused.

Nepherin was laughing, frantically, ignoring whatever fate awaited him. "Gaze beyond the abyss! But take care not to gaze for too long, for it is a steep fall, Titanlord, a steep fall indeed!"

Griffyn grinned and swung his sword. Nepherin's head rolled to the ground. Would the night be over? Severed with the King of the Gods?

He dropped to his knees and couldn't help the tears running down his cheeks. "I hope you were watching Rory, Vendel, and you too Ben... I hope you saw this," he said as his voice broke.

He shouted at the top of his lungs. Nepherin's body began to radiate a golden aura as it turned slowly to ashes.

Griffyn gawked and his pupils dilated. He quickly rose to his feet and swung the Masamune so hard that it punctured a hole in the wall. The ashes of Nepherin passed through a gazing red light.

"I will end you all, I swear it... This doesn't end here...Do you hear me!"

"Griffyn!" Natasha barged in and slid towards him, hugging him tightly. Her gaze quickly fell at the hole in the wall. A sort of glittering ashes passing around her. "What happened?"

Griffyn couldn't speak. He remained silent.

"The sky, Griffyn... the sky's turned red..."

# ACKNOWLEDGEMENTS

Wow, it took me 2 years to publish this. I want you to know, that almost half of this was done within a few months. I have no excuse for taking 2 years to publish it (I mean, I did publish another book but what the hell).

So many people were part of this journey (I told you guys, I never said Veda, Pollus, Magnus only). So, a very special thanks goes to my editor Nicole Hames, Bedoor Khalaf, Mo. Shehab, Nathan Dosco, S. E. Davidson, Neda Jahrami, and a whole bunch of people without which, this book would've never seen the light of day -there's a pun here, but I won't spoil it. Read the book.

# THANKS FOR READING!

Please add a short review on Amazon or where you got this from and let me know your thought! Reviews help authors tremendously.

I hope Griffyn, Rory and Ben kept you entertained. In fact, if you'd like to begin another series, I left a short excerpt of Fortier: The Long Night. Visit Amazon if you liked it to start another adventure, and meet up with Alfred Zeidan, the strongest!

## STILL LOOKING FOR MORE?

Make sure you subscribe to my newsletter to stay in touch, and receive a free copy of Moonlight Symphony!

www.mgdarwish.com/newsletter

Thanks, and good luck!

## M.G. DARWISH

# AN EXCERPT FROM
# FORTIER
## THE LONG NIGHT

Overnight, the world had changed. With the fall of the Bertrams and the Zeidans, the two most prominent vampire families in the world were no more. The balance was tipped, there was chaos that emitted a darkness which surpassed even the blackest of nights.

My name is Alfred. Having just put an end to a gruesome war in the underground, there was only one place where the likes of me would find peace.

The light of the moon dazzled, brightly challenging the darkness. Joy and empathy surrounded the place whilst caravans populated my surroundings.

"Daddy, Daddy! Let's go see the witch!" I heard a boy say to his father.

Witches? There is no such thing, and if there were, they wouldn't be so stupid to come here of all places... to exercise their gift so openly and so soon after the Salem Witch Trials would be idiotic.

"Alright, alright, calm down. We'll go see her after we find your mother, okay?" the dad replied.

# FORTIER: THE LONG NIGHT

I was intrigued.

Maybe it was time to pay this witch a visit.

Took me a good minute to find the tent. A sign next to it read 'Get your palm read at the low cost of five dollars!' Well, let's hop right in and see what the future holds for the likes of me.

I pushed aside the curtain and ducked inside. Dimly lit, mostly by candles. It smelled fresh. And sweaty. The humid weather made the air hot and stifling, not helped by the fact that most residents of Texas could do with a shower.

"You don't have a fate line," I heard the witch say to a guy who was sitting right across her.

"What does that mean?"

"It means you're in total control of your destiny."

"So, she's bound to say 'yes' eventually? Is that what you're telling me?" The man leaned forward eagerly. Hopeless romantic, or a creepy stalker? Anyway...

"That's exactly what I'm telling you." She paused as she turned her head towards me. "I'll be right with you darling, take a seat please."

"Yeah, you should wait for your turn—" started the other guy.

"Actually, there's nothing more to tell."

"But I have so many questions! How many kids will we have? When will we be able to move in together, seeing as her father is forbidding us to meet and talk most of the time—"

"Jack, you're in total control of your destiny," she said with a grim smile on her face. I wasn't sure which was more pathetic. To be so gullible as to take mere broad suggestions as facts, or the constant need to feed their ego.

"Alright, thank you, thank you so much! You've rekindled my—"

"Jack, I have other people to help."

"Alright, I won't keep you." He smiled from ear to ear. Definitely a stalker, I decided. Her father doesn't want them to talk or meet? Please... she probably didn't have the heart to tell him to piss off. How much simpler the world would be if humans accepted that as enough reason to back off.

"Sorry for the wait. Here, come sit here."

I looked at her from the corner of my eye. "They say you're a witch."

"I read palms. I don't cast spells, that would be silly, wouldn't it? But I guess the hopeless need a reason to keep believing when all hope is gone."

"So, you admit you tell them bullshit?"

The witch smiled. "Think of it as a placebo effect. They pay me to say what they want to hear. Now if that is wrong, then let he without sin cast the first stone."

"Funny. Quoting Jesus of Nazareth."

"What we do is somewhat the same."

"Not quite." I took a seat.

"What's your name?"

"Alfred."

"Just Alfred?"

"Yes."

"A mystery, eh?" She scratched her chin, taking my palm and laying it in front of her magic crystal. What horse shit. "Well, it's not entirely bullshit, but there is some science behind it. See this line?" She pointed at a line that stretched from the end of my right hand to the middle. "This is called the heart line. The more the markings on it, the more it symbolizes troubles with a loved one."

I shook my head. "Haven't been down that road for a long time."

"How long is a long time?"

"Would you believe me if I told you?"

"Are you asking if I would believe that you're a vampire?"

I leaned back in my chair as the witch assessed me.

"Hollow yellow eyes, six feet tall, broad shoulders and a long light brown robe. Word travels fast y'know, and you're not exactly inconspicuous. You're on everyone's radar now, you know," she said as she smirked at me.

"So, you are a witch."

"People call others witches or wizards because they see them do something that they cannot understand. In my case, all it takes is a good memory and a desire to see patterns."

"You're telling me, that all that there is to you is intense research on matters and individuals?"

She nodded.

"Some would call you a stalker."

"They can call me what they want," she laughed. "Now, why don't you ask what you're really here to ask?"

"If you're so good at what you do, then you should already know why I'm here."

"Seeing as you have just butchered—"

"Might want to skip those details. Not in the mood to revisit the past."

"And why is that?"

"Because the past is the past. Any who desire to dwell on it can read history books. I'm here right now to deal with the present. So that a bleak future does not stay atop our heads for very long."

"I don't know where you can find the Elders. But I know what can help you find one."

"I'm listening."

"Before this long night is passed, I'll need you to do something for me. Would you at least consider that? After you get what you want, of course."

"I'll think about it."

"I suppose that's as good as I'll get." She placed her hand on the magic crystal, closing her eyes and mumbling a few words. "Your future is bleak. It is filled with greatness, yet at a great cost. You will accomplish what you want. But only after you pay a hefty price."

"Not in the mood for puzzles, witch."

"I see something. A stone. Shiny, bright but dark. No, it does not shine bright, it shines... dark. It is vile and houses treachery. The creature that has it... is spoken of in legends—"

Sweat beaded on her forehead as she began to shake.

"What else?" I asked, curious to know what path would lead me to the dawn of a new world.

"That is all I can see." She opened her eyes. The shaking stopped but she was gasping for air as if she had just run a marathon. "That is all that I have for you."

"Are you sure that this will set me on the path that I want?"

"Of that, I am certain. All the signs are there. But I honestly don't know the correlation of the stone and that thing that houses it — that is mentioned in legends of course. I see a rose. It's lightly blue of some sort, does that make sense to you?"

I got up from the chair. "It's fine. I know."

"Wait," she said, rising. "You promised you'd hear my request, didn't you?"

I paused, not turning around. "I'm listening."

"There's a vampire nest, right here in this carnival. They organize it in every town so they can lure innocent humans and drink their blood."

"There are dozens of them, and only one of me."

"Please..." she begged.

I raised my eyebrows. "It's all a game to them, isn't it?"

"One that I want you to stop. I'm their prisoner, you know. In fact, they've been listening all along. They keep tabs on me."

And as if on cue, shouting and screaming burst from outside the tent. A clever ploy if I daresay myself.

"And why haven't you run already?"

"Because I'd never escape."

I sighed and kept walking. I could hear her heartbeat speed up. For someone who knew so much about the mysticism of the future, it was intriguing that she didn't think I'd help.

As I walked outside, the dim lighting of the tent was replaced by fire and fury. Vampires were latching onto anything alive that carried their precious water of life. I kept my pace, and slowly approached them.

Their eyes met mine.

# FORTIER: THE LONG NIGHT

"You... what the fuck... why the fuck are you here... shit," one of them said, dropping the body from which he was drinking. Blood covered his mouth to his neck.

It was a disturbing look, if I'm honest.

It took the rest of the group seconds to join in. "I'm not interested in you. I'm looking for the one who turned you all," I said calmly as I kept my pace walking towards them.

"Shit... shit... we're screwed..."

"Did you honestly think your tale had a happy ending?"

"Run! Run or we'll all die... it's the Fortier!"

# ABOUT THE AUTHOR

**M.G. Darwish** is an award nominated author who writes dark, twisted and action-packed fiction. He tries his best not to base his characters on anyone he knows in real life to avoid that extra weird conversation about how they were brutalized and killed in the book. Oh, and he's terrified of a penguin uprising more than ghosts and demons.

## CONNECT WITH M.G. DARWISH

**Twitter:** @infrangilis

**Instagram:** @infrangilis

www.mgdarwish.com

CPSIA information can be obtained
at www.ICGtesting.com
Printed in the USA
BVHW081553151020
591119BV00003B/176